"I thought you wanted me,"

Claren said as she traced the harshly cut line of his lips with a seashell-pink-tinted fingernail.

Dash grasped the tops of her arms. Whether to push her away or draw her closer, he didn't know. "Wanting and having are two different things. Dammit, Irish, this can't go anywhere."

The way this man could make her feel, with a single touch, a lingering look, was like nothing Claren had ever known. She had to take advantage of the emotions sparking between them *now*, before he moved on.

"I'd say it already has." She brushed her lips against his.

Dash told himself he was a fool for turning down what she was so willingly offering. But he'd come to realize that this was not the type of woman a man could easily walk away from.

She was scattering kisses from one corner of his mouth to the other. "Claren, there are a million reasons why this is wrong."

"I want to break all the rules with you, Dash."

Aching, he pulled her closer. "Damn you, Irish," he groaned as his mouth savaged hers. *The hell with the rule*

Dear Reader,

Temptation is Harlequin's boldest, most sensuous romance series . . . a series for the 1990s! Fast-paced, humorous, adventurous, these stories are about men and women falling in love—and making the ultimate commitment.

Nineteen ninety-two marked the debut of Rebels & Rogues, our yearlong salute to the Temptation hero. In these twelve exciting books—one a month—by popular authors, including Jayne Ann Krentz, Ruth Jean Dale and Janice Kaiser, you'll meet men like Josh—who swore *never* to play the hero. Trey—he lived life on the edge . . . and wasn't about to be tamed by a beautiful woman. Alex—hot on the trail of the biggest story of his career until he was KO'd by a knockout . . . Gabriella.

Twelve rebels and rogues—men who are rough around the edges, but incredibly sexy. Men full of charm, yet ready to fight for the love of a very special woman. . . .

I hope you enjoy Rebels & Rogues, plus all the other terrific Temptation novels coming in 1992!

Warm regards,

Birgit Davis-Todd
Senior Editor

P.S. We love to hear from our readers!

THE KNIGHT IN SHINING ARMOR

JoANN ROSS

Harlequin Books

TORONTO • NEW YORK • LONDON
AMSTERDAM • PARIS • SYDNEY • HAMBURG
STOCKHOLM • ATHENS • TOKYO • MILAN
MADRID • WARSAW • BUDAPEST • AUCKLAND

Published September 1992

ISBN 0-373-25509-8

THE KNIGHT IN SHINING ARMOR

1

DASH MACKENZIE HAD long ago come to the conclusion that there was nothing left in the world that would surprise him. That was before he saw Claren Wainwright racing toward him down the quiet, tree-shaded street of Seattle, Washington, the cathedral-length satin train of her wedding dress trailing in the dust behind her.

Vaguely amused, he drove past the formally dressed young woman, made a U-turn and pulled the rental car up alongside her.

She'd slowed to a swift walk. When she heard the sound of an automatic window rolling down, Claren glanced at the car, frowned, then, directing her gaze straight ahead again, walked even faster.

"Can I offer you a lift?"

"Thanks. But I don't accept rides from strangers." She didn't slow down, nor did she look at him.

Her veil was a billowy white cloud, hiding her face from Dash's view. Her stride was surprisingly lengthy, considering her lack of height, as if she was determined to make up in assertiveness what she lacked in stature.

"That's wise," he agreed. "But I'm not a stranger. Not really."

Claren shifted her heavy, oversize tote bag from one shoulder to the other and wished he'd leave her alone. Hadn't she already had enough trouble for one day?

"That's what they all say." She shot him a quick, irritated look. "If you're that anxious to pick up a woman, why don't you go downtown and try one of the hotels? The Sheraton, perhaps. Or the Hilton. They both get a lot of convention trade."

"I realize that I'm a bit rusty on the logistics of picking up women," Dash said. "But what's the advantage of convention trade?"

"According to an article I read in the *Hotelier's Journal*, there are a great many women who attend conventions to have wild flings with men they wouldn't look at twice back home."

"Fascinating."

"Isn't it?"

Although she refused to slow down, Claren couldn't help noticing that his drawled tone was husky and undoubtedly appealing to most women. She might even find it alluring, if she was interested. Which she definitely was not.

"There's a convention of female wrestlers in town this weekend," she informed him briskly. "Perhaps you'll get lucky."

Nerve, Dash thought. The woman certainly had more than her share of that. "I think I already have."

Claren stopped in her tracks, put her hands on her satin-and-lace covered hips and turned toward him.

She drew in a soft, involuntary breath as she found herself looking straight into a compelling, hard-hitting face with absolutely no softening features. His skin— tanned to a deep, rich mahogany—was stretched tight over strong bones, his nose was as sharp and as straight as a blade, his mouth was a harsh slash. His hair was as sleek and black as a raven's wing.

He was wearing aviator-style sunglasses, which kept her from viewing his eyes, but Claren knew he was examining her. She shivered.

"This is ridiculous." Claren shook her head, causing a few errant strands of wavy hair to tumble free from beneath the pearl tiara capping her billowy veil. "I don't know why I'm even talking to you."

Darcy had always called her beautiful. But now, as his gaze skimmed her face, Dash decided the older man had been prejudiced. Because Claren Wainwright wasn't conventionally beautiful at all.

Her face was too narrow—all bones and hollows— and her chin, which she was presently jutting his way, was too sharp. Her lips were a shade too full, the set of her mouth blatantly stubborn.

Not that the woman was without feminine assets. Her complexion was incredible—a milky porcelain that painters love and most women curse. And her eyes! They were wide and thickly lashed, with all the forty shades of Ireland green swirling in their depths. At the moment those incredible eyes were spitting furious emerald sparks his way.

"Maybe you're willing to talk to me because you don't want to walk all the way to—" Dash paused. "Where are you going, anyway?"

"Good question."

Now that he mentioned it, Claren realized she should have given more thought to her behavior. But escape had taken top priority.

"There's always your uncle's house," he suggested.

That quiet comment earned her immediate attention. "How do you know about that?"

"Darcy and I are—were," he corrected, "friends." Keeping his eyes on her face, Dash stuck his hand out the window. "I'm Dashiell MacKenzie," he introduced himself. "My friends call me Dash."

Claren recognized the name immediately. Hadn't it been scrawled at the bottom of the single-page document leaving all Darcy O'Neill's possessions to his only living relative, Claren O'Neill Wainwright? Unable to stand still, when her nerves were still jumping around like a cat on a griddle, Claren lifted her snowy skirts and started walking again.

"You witnessed my uncle's will." It still hurt; Claren supposed it always would.

Dash kept the car at a crawl in order to keep the conversation going and wished he could see the legs hidden by that voluminous skirt. "Guilty," he said. "Although at the time neither of us realized how soon he was going to need it."

Ever since the day he'd gotten the news of Darcy O'Neill's "accident," Dash had wondered if Darcy had known a lot more than he'd been telling. Like the little fact that Darcy had gotten himself in more trouble than he could handle.

Claren glanced over at him. She wished she could see his eyes. "Seattle isn't exactly around the corner from Jamaica."

Her uncle, artist turned amateur archaeologist, treasure seeker and lifetime victim of wanderlust, had been living on the Caribbean island until just two short weeks ago. It was where he'd died. Although his body had not been recovered, his boat had been found abandoned six miles from the treacherous reefs surrounding the island.

Since several sunken treasure galleons dating back to the Spanish Armada were rumored to be in the area, and Darcy had been bragging about sunken hoards of silver and gold and jewels in every saloon on the island, authorities—accustomed to dealing with wide-eyed dreamers who chased the ghost ships resting on the ocean floor of the New World—had written his death off as yet another unfortunate drowning accident.

"So what could possibly be important enough to bring you all this way?" Claren asked.

"That should be obvious. I came to see you."

A sudden light gust of wind blew the diaphanous veil against her cheek. She pushed the tulle out of the way with an irritated gesture. Dash could almost see the fiery aura of impatience shimmering around her.

"Why?"

She wasn't going to be a pushover. For some reason he'd take time to figure out later, Dash liked the idea that Darcy O'Neill's beloved niece was more than just a pretty face.

"Because Darcy loved you. And because he talked about you a lot. And because I have a personal item of his I felt belonged to you."

"You could have mailed it."

"True. But then I would have missed your wedding."

Vivid color—whether guilt or embarrassment, Dash couldn't discern—rose in her cheeks. "There's not going to be a wedding."

Dash was curious, but decided he could wait for that little tale. "Too bad."

Claren thought she detected humor in his drawled statement. She searched for a sign that he was laughing at her and was mildly frustrated when she couldn't find it. "It was all for the best."

"Whatever you say."

A truck loaded with freshly cut logs came up behind them. The driver, a burly, sunburned man wearing a red-and-black-plaid shirt, rolled down his window.

"Hey, lady," he called out to Claren, "is that guy hassling you?"

He was. But looking at the lumberman's bulging biceps, Claren realized that if she told the truth, she'd be responsible for starting a brawl. Which, after the day she'd already had, was simply more than she could handle.

"No. Really, everything's fine," she said at the trucker's disbelieving look.

He looked from her to Dash's unreadable face, then back again. "You sure?"

No. She wasn't. In fact, she was about as far from fine as she'd been for a very long time. But Claren didn't feel like getting into an extended conversation with yet another stranger. Instead, she flashed the driver a reassuring smile.

"Positive. But thank you so very much for asking."

Giving the pair one last curious look, the man pulled the truck around Dash's car and continued down the winding road, headed toward the waterfront docks, taking the pungent scent of freshly cut Douglas fir with him.

"I know you said you didn't want a ride, but it's a long walk back to Queen Anne Hill," Dash reminded her. "Especially in a wedding gown and high heels."

A frisson of fear skimmed up her spine, and for an instant Claren found herself wishing she hadn't sent the lumberman away. "How do you know where I live?"

"I told you, I was a friend of Darcy's. He read me all your letters."

"Oh." Even as Claren admitted that made sense, she couldn't keep the lingering suspicion from her voice.

"Perhaps these will vouch for me," Dash said.

He held out a small photo album. Claren flipped through the pages, stopping when she got to a well-worn picture of a man and a young girl. The girl's dress was a froth of white; the mass of red-gold hair under the short veil looked as if it had never known a comb. Cracks nearly obliterated the man's features, but Claren didn't need to see his face to recognize the picture.

"This was taken the day of my first holy communion," she murmured. "Back in Ireland." Her eyes grew reminiscent as bittersweet memories flooded over her.

"That's how I recognized you. From the dress," Dash explained at her questioning glance. "It's a lot like the one you're wearing today."

Claren looked down, surprised by his perceptive comment. Her wedding gown was, indeed, fashioned along the lines of the remarkable dress her uncle had bought her from America so many years ago. Which, she supposed, explained why she'd fallen in love with the gown at first sight, despite the fact that its frothy romantic style—a style Scarlett O'Hara would have probably done murder for—was a distinct contrast to the starkly tailored clothing she usually favored.

"I suppose it is," she murmured, flipping through the pages. The final photo was a picture of her uncle Darcy, taken in the company of another man. Darcy's wild red beard was streaked with gray, revealing that this photo had been taken more recently. Although the eyes of her uncle's companion were shielded by a pair of mirrored sunglasses that reflected a pair of palm trees, Claren would have recognized the unforgiving lines of his face and that deep cleft in the man's chin anywhere.

"These only demonstrate that you knew my uncle," she said. "It doesn't prove that you were friends."

Frustration warred with admiration. Dash recognized Claren Wainwright's hard-headed attitude. Hadn't he witnessed the same stubborn behavior from her uncle more times than he cared to count?

"How about this?"

Another car passed them, this one a sporty red convertible. The two teenage boys inside the car wolf-whistled as they roared by. Eager to be on her way, Claren snatched the envelope from his outstretched hand.

It was a letter, written in her uncle's nearly illegible scrawl. It was, however, lacking Darcy O'Neill's characteristically Irish, lavishly exaggerated, prose. The message was brief almost to the point of being curt, as if he'd been in a hurry.

My darling Claren,
If you're reading this, it means that my luck has finally run out and I've bought a one-way ticket to Davy Jones's locker. Dash might not be what you're accustomed to, but he's a good man. In his own way. Trust him.

Love, your uncle, Darcy

Claren glanced up at Dash. "Do you know what this says?"

"The envelope is sealed," Dash pointed out. It was a problem he'd gotten around easily.

Once again Claren wished that he'd take off the damn glasses. His answer was less than candid—if only she could see his eyes. "He's telling me to trust you," she revealed. "What do you think that means?"

Dash had been asking himself that same question for the past two weeks, ever since the letter had shown up in his mail—along with another from Darcy, requesting he take the letter to Claren in Seattle—postmarked the day Darcy had disappeared.

"Perhaps he's talking about letting me drive you back to your apartment."

It was more than that. But whatever her uncle was referring to, Claren was in no mood to figure it out. "There's no point in going there," she informed him. "I sold the apartment and since it closed escrow two weeks early, I moved in with my aunt and uncle."

Dash knew that. "Why not with your fiancé?" It was a question that had been bothering him for two weeks.

"Elliott felt that wouldn't be proper." Claren was surprised to hear herself reveal such a personal fact to a total stranger. "He was worried that people would talk."

She frowned as she remembered how he'd gone on in great length to explain that openly living together could endanger his plans for a political career.

"If I wanted a woman badly enough to marry her, I damn well wouldn't let her sleep at some relatives' house," Dash said. "I'd keep her in my bed. Where she belonged."

Before Claren could respond to that blatantly chauvinistic statement, he said, "Elliott, I take it, was to be the groom."

Actually Darcy had told him all about Claren's fiancé, and what he'd had to say was a great deal less than flattering. Dash, however, kept his knowledge to himself.

"Yes." Claren sighed, trying to ignore how his statement about a woman's place being in a man's bed had made her blood hot. "He'll probably never forgive me for embarrassing him in front of all those Byrds."

A little voice in the back of her mind reminded Claren that Elliott had deserved it. But at the moment that didn't make her feel any better about leaving three hundred wedding guests waiting in her aunt's rose garden.

"Birds?"

"Byrds," Claren corrected, spelling it out for him. "That's his family. They all came." Another sigh. "Hundreds of them." She glanced back over her shoulder, as if expecting to see flocks of formally dressed individuals descending on her.

"You could always check into the Palace," Dash suggested.

Seattle's Whitfield Palace Hotel. Home of the advertising slogan, When Deluxe Will No Longer Do. Claren had worked at the hotel since her graduation from University of Washington four years earlier—a year ahead of the rest of her class—starting out as a customer-relations liaison and swiftly working her way up to night manager.

"I quit my job." Elliott hadn't wanted his wife working all night while he was home alone. Claren, wanting to avoid yet another argument over the subject, had finally complied. Like a fool.

"I see."

Claren had the strange feeling that he did and was grateful when he didn't comment on what she suspected was a very wrong decision.

"It seems you've burned a great many bridges." When Claren didn't immediately answer, Dash said, "There's always Darcy's house."

Her uncle Darcy's house. That wonderful, sprawling place—which Claren had inherited—in the Victorian peninsula town of Port Vancouver. But there were strings accompanying her uncle's inheritance. Strings that had made it impossible to accept. Until now. A reckless, enormously appealing idea stirred at the back of her mind.

"I put it up for sale," she admitted.

Dash wasn't surprised. "I told Darcy that's what you'd do."

Claren lifted a brow. "Oh?" The single word dripped with scorn.

There was a challenge in her tone that reminded Dash of her uncle. Right before Darcy's fiery Irish temper would explode.

"To hear your uncle tell it, you have a pretty good life," he said. "A prestigious job at one of the most luxurious hotel chains in the world, an apartment on pricey Queen Anne Hill with a view of Puget Sound, a recession-proof stock portfolio, a trendy European sedan and annual trips to Europe and Hawaii."

"The car was a company car, the portfolio has suffered some rather demoralizing losses lately, I no longer have either my job or my apartment and the trips were all business related, reimbursed by Whitfield Palace Hotels. And how do you know so much about me, anyway?" Although she'd begun to relax, that question had her feeling uneasy all over again.

"I told you, Darcy talked about you a lot. Which is why I said it was crazy to think you'd toss all that away. Just for a house."

Claren tilted her chin. A faint, stubborn line appeared between her tawny brows. "It's not just a house." From the time she'd moved to the United States, Darcy's sprawling residence had been the closest thing Claren had known to a real home. Her decision was made.

"I'll take you up on that offer of a ride after all," she declared.

"Terrific." Dash reached over and opened the passenger door. "Where are we going?" he asked.

Claren didn't disappoint him. After settling into the passenger seat with a flurry of lace and satin, she said, "To Port Vancouver."

2

HER SOFT SCENT WAS reminiscent of a summer meadow—blooming with lavender and wildflowers, and warmed by a bright buttery sun. It filled the car like a fragrant cloud, more aura than perfume. Against his will, Dash found himself drawn to it. To her. Frowning, he reminded himself that he was here to do a job; he hadn't come all this way to start behaving like some libidinous teenager.

"Want to stop at your aunt and uncle's and pick up some things on the way?"

"That's not necessary," she said quickly.

Too quickly, Dash thought, sensing the reason for her reluctance. So, she wasn't entirely fearless. He'd have to keep that little fact in mind.

"I have my makeup in my bag. As for clothes and toiletries, I can buy whatever I need on the peninsula and send for the rest of my things later."

That was the truth, so far as it went. But if she were to be perfectly honest, Claren would have to admit that after the way she'd ruined the wedding—a ceremony that had been twelve months in the planning—she was not all that eager to risk running into her Aunt Winifred and Uncle Richard.

Although she'd tried for years to avoid doing anything to earn their disapproval, she knew she would never forget their icy reaction to her news that she could not—would not—marry Elliott Byrd as planned.

"Whatever you say," Dash said agreeably. He wasn't about to push. She had, after all, had a rather eventful day, and he understood her reluctance.

Without seeming to take his eyes off the road, he glanced surreptitiously down at his watch. Damn. It was past time to check in. St. John had always been a stickler for punctuality, which just went to show how much the guys in the pin-striped suits knew about the unpredictability of this kind of work.

"I've got to stop and get some cigarettes."

"That's fine with me," Claren answered absently as she struggled to extract the long hairpins holding her tiara in place.

He pulled into the parking lot of a drugstore.

"Can I get you anything?"

"No, thanks." She tossed the gossamer veil into the back seat. "I'll wait to go shopping until we get to Port Vancouver."

Claren sighed as she thought about all she'd left behind. It was a great deal more than clothing—that could be easily replaced, after all. What had her feeling so sad was the knowledge she'd also turned her back on all that was left of her family. She was, truly, all alone.

"You know, as hard as it is to believe, one of these days you'll be able to laugh about this."

His mouth curved in the barest hint of a smile, and although the glasses still hid his eyes from her view, Claren thought she detected honest concern in his tone. "I keep telling myself that."

"If nothing else, running away from the altar will make a hell of a story to tell your grandchildren."

Her appreciative laughter bubbled free, like the fresh clarity of a mountain spring.

Frowning at the way that clear sound had pulled some hidden chord deep inside him, Dash left the car and went into the store. Ignoring the clerk who was standing at the front counter, he headed straight to the back wall, where the pay phones were located.

Dash looked around the store, ensuring no one was within hearing distance. Other than the clerk, the only customer in the store was a harried-looking young woman with a baby waiting at the prescription counter. The baby, obviously ill, was fretful, his strident cries ensuring that neither the pharmacist nor the mother could overhear Dash's conversation. A glance out the front window showed Claren sitting in the car where he'd left her.

He dialed, then deposited the required change into the slot.

The phone was picked up on the first ring.

"I've made contact," he said.

The voice on the other end of the long-distance line asked a question.

"No, she doesn't suspect a thing. And we hit a piece of luck—she's going to be staying at the house."

The heated response came quick and hard, like machine-gun fire.

"Calm down, St. John, I didn't blow my cover. She came up with the idea all on her own. It turns out that since she'd planned to get married, she'd moved out of her own apartment and needed a place to stay."

St. John asked a question, his voice calmer now.

"No. The wedding was called off. So we're all set. Okay," he said, "I'll call you when I get to the house."

CLAREN CLOSED her eyes and leaned her head against the back of the seat. She still couldn't believe what she'd done. But that didn't mean that she regretted her actions. Not even the teeniest bit. After what Elliott had done, after the lies he'd told, not to mention his treacherous betrayal, she should have pushed the cheating, unfaithful bastard, white tie and all, right into Lake Washington.

When she'd first arrived in America from County Clare, Ireland, after her parents' deaths to live with an aunt she'd never met, Claren had been twelve years old. She'd also been heartbroken, frightened and unbearably lonely.

Although Winifred Wainwright Palmer had been nice enough, in a smooth, polite way, and had seen to all Claren's physical needs, she kept an emotional distance from her young niece that was worlds apart from the unqualified love Claren had received from her mother and father.

Just when she thought she was going to shrivel up and die from loneliness, Elliott Byrd, the son of her aunt's best friend and next-door neighbor, had stepped in to smooth the way.

Seven years older than Claren, tall, blond and unbelievably handsome, Elliott, who was home for summer vacation after his freshman year at Harvard, quickly became her protector, her knight in shining armor.

Not embarrassed to be seen with a little girl, he'd allowed her to tag along to the movies and later to the pizza place with his friends, who inevitably had quit grousing and had become accustomed to having the young Irish girl around.

Three blissful months later, Elliott had returned to college, leaving Claren bereft. She'd missed him terribly. Being young and incredibly naive, she'd written him long, impassioned letters, spilling her turmoiled emotions onto every page.

Instead of laughing at her or treating her with disdain, Elliott had simply suggested Claren would do well to learn to control her emotions. Having taken a genetics class his first semester, he understood that her Irish ancestry—from her mother's branch of her family tree—tended to make her feelings closer to the surface. But after all, he'd written, she was in America now, and such tempers and emotional outbursts were perceived by most individuals in their social stratum to be unattractive. And immature.

It was the same thing her aunt had been telling her. And although Claren had tried her best to control her unruly emotions, inevitably the pressure would build up and she'd just have to explode, like one of the volcanoes that continued to rumble ominously in the Northwest's Cascade Mountains.

It was like asking a fish not to swim. A bird not to fly. Or trying to insist that the sun stop coming up every morning. But hopelessly in love with Elliott, Claren had thrown herself into a self-improvement course that would have made a convent-trained German nun seem reckless by comparison. She had been determined to become a proper American lady, a lady suitable for the title of Mrs. Elliott Byrd.

Her hard work had paid off. By the time she was in her final year at the University of Washington, Claren O'Neill Wainwright had become a near clone of Winifred Wainwright Palmer, her proper-society matron aunt. And although her uncle Darcy loudly and continually insisted that she was shutting off the best part of herself, Claren was satisfied with the serene, sophisticated young woman who looked back at her from the dressing-table mirror every morning.

As a reward for such selfless effort, Elliott had made eight years of Claren's fervent wishes come true by telling her that her love was not one-sided.

They had announced their engagement in June, a year after she'd graduated from college with a degree in hotel management. Elliott was working for a Seattle brokerage house. Both the Palmer and the Byrd families, who'd been watching the evolving romance for years, had professed delight.

That had been three long years ago. It certainly hadn't been Claren's idea to wait. But Elliott had patiently explained that during those initial years at the brokerage house, he needed to devote a major portion of both his time and his energy to his work. He was, he told her, determined to make partner before he turned thirty. Then he was going to throw his hat into the Washington State political ring.

When he asked Claren how she'd like being the wife of a U.S. senator, she'd answered honestly: whatever made him happy, made her happy. When he'd assured her that she'd love living in the nation's capital, having dinner at the White House with the president and first lady, Claren's agreement had been a bit less enthusiastic.

Although she'd come a long way from the Irish country girl she once was, formal dinner parties—stiffly proper society events of any kind—always made her feel as if her stomach had been turned into a wildlife refuge for giant condors.

Elliott had made partner, exactly as he planned, a week before his thirtieth birthday. Shortly thereafter, rumors of his candidacy had begun appearing in the local papers. Everything was going precisely according to schedule. Finally, as he'd promised, he'd instructed Claren to set the date for their wedding.

Having already waited too long, Claren had wanted to get married as soon as the state of Washington would allow. That's when both mothers had quickly stepped in, reminding her that the families were descendants of early Seattle settlers. As such, they had a certain obligation to uphold tradition. Besides, Mrs. Byrd had pointed out, community interest in the event would certainly not harm Elliott's budding political career.

Reluctantly Claren had acquiesced, allowing her aunt and future mother-in-law to plan an "appropriate wedding." That had been twelve long months ago, and with each passing day, the upcoming nuptials had become more and more lavish, until they rivaled the marriage of Prince Charles and Lady Di. On more than one occasion, a frustrated Claren had accused her aunt of trying to outdo the British royal family.

The wedding was to have taken place in the formal gardens behind her aunt's mock Tudor lakefront home. A trio of gardeners had been working overtime to ensure that every one of the red and white rosebushes would be in full bloom for the ceremony. The dark green rolling lawns, trimmed to perfection, rivaled a putting green. Peacocks, hired solely for the occasion, strolled that luxurious lawn, displaying their feathers.

Folding chairs—three hundred of them, their seats covered in white satin—had been set up in neat rows on the croquet green facing the gazebo, where Claren and Elliott were to have taken their vows. Nearby, sheltered by a white tent, were damask-draped tables groaning with gourmet delights and bottles of imported champagne.

At the front of the tent, tall sterling-silver urns were filled with small squares of spicy groom's cake, wrapped in white tissue and tied with gold ribbons, intended as favors for the guests.

The wedding cake, displayed on a table by itself, consisting of nine towering layers of white cake topped with buttercream frosting, was surrounded by white roses. A porcelain bride and groom—created by a local artist and wearing Claren and Elliott's faces—stood atop the cake. As a final touch, the tiny bride's dress was a replica of Claren's own bridal gown.

"It was just like a three-ring circus," Claren complained now.

"What did you say?" Dash, who'd returned to the car, asked.

Having been immersed in her unhappy thoughts, Claren had failed to notice his arrival. "My aunt Winifred rented a tent for the reception."

Dash, remembering the outrageous dog-and-pony show that had been his own formal wedding, frowned. "That's not so unusual. In certain circles."

There was something in his tone Claren couldn't quite discern. Sarcasm? Anger? Resentment? Shrugging it off, she said, "I know. But it still seemed more like a circus than a proper wedding."

"I can understand why you'd feel that way."

Growing up poor, never knowing where his next meal would come from, forced to accept the charity of others in order to survive, Dash had spent years planning his escape.

Success. Money. Fame. As a boy, he'd thirsted for those elusive goals in the same way a parched man crawling across the Sahara Desert yearns for a drink of cool clear water. As a man, he'd learned the hard way to be very careful what you wished for.

"But it's a moot point now," he said gruffly, angry at the way she'd unearthed long-ago memories he'd spent a lifetime trying to bury. "Unless you're going to change your mind again."

Claren didn't like the challenge in his tone. "Not on a bet."

Not if Elliott Byrd crawled across a bed of hot coals on his hands and knees. Not if he quit his precious job at the brokerage house, bought a boat and invited her to sail off with him to the South Seas, where they could spend the rest of their days making love and feeding one another passion fruit.

Not even—and this would be a hard one to resist— if he bought back the O'Neills' old horse farm overlooking the Shannon River in Ireland's County Clare for a wedding present.

Dash heard both the anger and the hurt in her voice and narrowed his eyes. But he didn't comment.

"Hey," he answered with a shrug as he pulled the car into the flow of late-afternoon rush-hour traffic, "it's your life."

Thirty minutes later Claren was standing at the railing of a ferry slowly making its way across Puget Sound. The stiff breeze coming off the water tore at her formally coiffed hair and ruffled her satin skirts. Feeling wonderfully, blessedly free for the first time in months, Claren faced the wind straight on.

"It would be a lot warmer indoors," Dash suggested, nodding toward the glassed-in enclosure.

Her attention on a pair of pelicans perched atop wooden pilings, Claren didn't look at him. "True. But it wouldn't be nearly as much fun."

Fun. When had it become such an alien word? she wondered. And knew the answer—ever since her parents had died in an auto accident returning from a successful day at the Ballinasloe horse fair, forcing her to leave the only home she'd ever known, the home she loved, to live with her father's sister. From the time Claren was twelve years old, the only real fun in her admittedly comfortable existence had been those wonderful, unexpected visits from her uncle Darcy. But now he was gone and Claren felt as if he'd taken all the sunshine with him.

Sighing, she leaned against the railing. The setting sun had turned the water a shimmering copper.

Although you couldn't tell it from the temperature out on the water, it was June. The ferry's inside observation decks were crowded with vacationers and office workers commuting back home from the city.

A pair of boys—nine-year-old twins from the look of them—raced each other down the outside deck, oblivious to the frustrated shouts of their mother. The harried woman rushed past Dash, skidding to a stop long enough to take a startled look at Claren, still clad in her snowy bridal attire. The boys had reached the back of the boat and were leaning far over the railing, pointing at something bobbing on the water. The woman cast a last puzzled look Claren's way, then took off running.

It was cold enough that everyone else had opted to stay indoors, leaving Dash and Claren alone on the deck. Dash leaned against the side of the boat and continued to watch her with an interest he tried to tell himself was purely professional.

But that didn't stop him from noticing that her cheeks, kissed by the salt breeze, bloomed with the hue of late-summer roses, or that her hair, tangled wildly by the breeze, was like no other color he'd ever seen. Too fiery for chestnut, lighter than titian, it was a rare blending of copper, gold and bronze.

"If you don't stop staring at me like that, I'm going to push you overboard," Claren said after he'd studied her for nearly ten minutes without saying a word.

Dash's grin was quick and arrogantly male. "I'm quaking in my boots."

She'd had a very trying day, and his sarcasm triggered a temper she'd spent the past twelve years suppressing. She spun around. "You should be," she retorted. "Because, for your information, Mr. Dashiell MacKenzie, I've taken judo—I could toss you right over that railing before you could say Jack Sprat."

Dash watched her face and found himself intrigued by the passion underlying the ivory and roses. He lifted a challenging brow. "Judo?"

"I have a brown belt. All the better to handle the likes of men like you."

He crossed the narrow width of the deck to her. "You know, Claren O'Neill Wainwright, there's a good deal of Ireland in your voice when you get your back up. Sure and it's a fine lesson in international cadence," he drawled in an exaggerated brogue. "You remind me of your uncle."

His eyes moved over her, from the top of her flame-colored head down to the white satin slippers peeking out from beneath her billowing skirts. "Except you're a hell of a lot prettier than old Darcy."

Claren shot him what she hoped was a lethal glare. "You are as mad as a hatter."

He took a step closer, enjoying the temper in her eyes. "And you are lovely."

He was a mere whisper away; his long legs, clad in black denim jeans, flattened the front of her skirt. Her fiery head barely skimmed his shoulder. Although he hadn't touched her, they both knew he would. They also knew what it would be like. Heat and smoke and passion.

Ignoring her scathing look, he reached out and wound a long strand of hair around his finger. "You're losing your pins."

Her pulse accelerated; her skin, despite the cold wind, heated. Claren suddenly felt as if she'd taken a long step backward, right off the slanting deck into the icy water.

Jerking free, she grasped the wayward curl from his hand, tucked it under the others atop her head and jabbed the pin painfully into her scalp. "I'm warning you—"

"I know." Unable to recall the last time he'd enjoyed himself more, Dash held up both hands, palms outward, in a gesture of self-defense. "The judo." His mocking grin suggested that he was a great deal less than terrified by Claren's threat. "Tell me, Irish," he said, "how tall are you? Five feet? Five feet one?"

Claren drew herself up to her full height. Even so, she had to tilt her head back to look into his face. "I'll have you know, I'm five foot two inches tall."

"That tall," Dash murmured. A hint of amusement touched his mouth. "Imagine. And you weigh, what, a hundred pounds?"

Claren hated the way he seemed to be enjoying himself at her expense. Her fingers were practically itching to hit something. Or someone. She curled them into a fist.

"One hundred and nine pounds. And a half."

"Without all those satin petticoats."

Damn the man. He had her there. "One hundred and three," she acknowledged reluctantly. "But size doesn't matter one little whit in judo. It's all a matter of technique."

He could challenge her. Even if Claren did know jujitsu, which he strongly doubted, she'd be no match for either his size or his skill. At the thought of her lying on her back on that worn wooden deck, surrounded by yards of satin and lace, vulnerable, yet with those incredible eyes shooting furious sparks, desire slammed into him.

Frowning, Dash forced it down. The woman, as intriguing as she seemed, was simply a job. Just like any other. It took an effort, but he almost made his head believe that. Unfortunately his rebellious body wasn't listening.

"For such a little thing, you sure as hell don't give anything away," he said. "Darcy always said that you were a spitfire."

Claren wanted to stay angry with him. But at the mention of her uncle, her fury melted away. "Uncle

Darcy always brought out the worst in me." Her soft smile warmed with tender reminiscence. "He was, of course, a rascal. Aunt Winifred always called him a black sheep."

Curious, she leaned back against the railing again and looked up at Dash, her eyes filled with questions. "How did you meet Darcy?"

He'd been waiting for that one and had his story ready. "I was living in Jamaica when he arrived chasing his ghost galleon. We ran into one another in a beachfront bar and hit it off right away."

That much, so far as it went, was the absolute truth. "You know how your uncle is. Was," Dash corrected, wondering how long it would take him to get used to the idea that Darcy was dead.

"Uncle Darcy never met a stranger," Claren agreed.

She thought of all the questions she wanted to ask. Things about Darcy, about his life, his dreams. She wanted to ask if her beloved uncle had still been a racing addict; she wanted to know if he had continued to drink two fingers, neat, of Irish every night before retiring. And most of all, she wanted to know if he'd been happy. At the end.

"You said you were living in Jamaica," she said instead.

Dash's antennae went up. "That's right."

"What do you do?"

"Do?"

"For a living."

"Oh." Dash's shoulders moved in a careless shrug. "A little of this. A little of that."

He was surprised when his vague answer earned another smile. "Another black sheep." For some reason Claren found that idea vaguely appealing.

"Yeah. I guess you could say that."

Her smile wavered, then turned a little sad. A shadow moved across her eyes. "I always wanted to be a black sheep."

"Don't look now," Dash suggested, "but I think you've just accomplished your wish."

Claren glanced down at the billowy skirt of her pearl-encrusted wedding dress, as if surprised to find herself still wearing it. She felt simultaneous feelings of annoyance and admiration; she did not like the idea of Dash MacKenzie reading her so well and so fast. But on the other hand, she couldn't help admiring his perception.

"I think you're right."

She looked back over her shoulder, where the sleek glass towers of the Seattle skyline were fading in the distance. And although she knew that she was being outrageously fanciful, Claren imagined that she could see all her burned bridges smoldering in ruins behind her.

3

PORT VANCOUVER, LOCATED on the far northeast corner of the Olympic Peninsula, resembled a small Victorian seaport. At the center of the town stood a tall clock tower that could be seen for miles.

Turreted, gingerbread-encrusted Victorian buildings, revealing the opulence and optimism of a bygone era, perched atop the tall bluff overlooking the Strait of Juan de Fuca. The broad, blue-green channel of water, separating the United States from Canada, flowed from Puget Sound to the Pacific. It was, Dash knew from his research, both wide enough—fourteen miles at the mouth—and deep enough to allow the navy's Trident submarines easy access to their base on the Hood Canal.

"It reminds me of New England," he said.

"Port Vancouver was settled by sea captains and merchants from back east," Claren told him.

She took a deep breath, drawing in the vigorous fresh air, the scent of saltwater, a distant biting aroma of fir and another scent she could not quite identify.

"At the end of the last century, the people all believed Port Vancouver was going to become the New York of the West," she said, watching a brown pelican winging its way along the coastline in search of fish. The awkward-looking bird was surprisingly graceful in flight.

The ferry was approaching the pier. When the docking call sounded, Claren and Dash returned to the car parked below deck.

"During its heyday, it was a port for merchant ships, whalers and even warships," Claren continued with the town's history as they waited in the car. "The old-timers, who can still remember the stories told by their parents and grandparents, love to tell tales about sailors being forcefully, or unknowingly, recruited from the local saloons and bordellos."

"Thanks to the ubiquitous Mickey Finn."

"I suppose so. When I first arrived in this country, fresh from my family's wee horse farm in County Clare, those stories seemed wonderfully romantic."

Dash kept his eyes on her face. "So you like romance. I should have guessed."

There was an accusatory edge to his deep, husky voice. The smile Claren had been about to give him never formed.

The ferry had docked; passengers and cars began to disembark.

"Guessed what?" she asked coolly.

"That a woman like you would be a sucker for sweet talk, flowers and candlelight."

Claren muttered a low sound of frustration. "You don't know what kind of woman I am."

"You're right about that, Irish." He gave her a bland smile that did nothing to lessen her annoyance. "But I will." Before she could give him a scathing answer, he said, "You were telling me about the town."

A thousand curses came to Claren's mind, including some in Gaelic that she'd been unaware of remembering. Refusing to let him know exactly how easily he could throw her off balance, Claren forced her mind back to her earlier subject.

"At any rate," she said, her words clipped with a lingering frustration she couldn't conceal, "when the word got out that there was going to be a railroad spur from Port Vancouver to the Union Pacific in Portland, which would make the town the premier port of the Northwest, all the citizens built warehouses and banks and those big, fine houses you can see up on the bluff."

Home, she realized suddenly as Dash drove the car off the ferry. That brisk, comforting aroma represented home.

"It was a remarkable boom," she continued. "The town's population doubled and redoubled."

"So what happened?"

Dash knew that, too. Her uncle had told him a lot about the town, and what Darcy hadn't mentioned, his research had revealed. But he liked the way her remarkable eyes lit up when she talked about the town. And, he admitted, he just liked hearing her talk, period.

Twelve years of living in the States had not entirely succeeded in ridding her speech of its soft Irish brogue. The sound of her voice brought up images of blue rivers curling like ribbons on the mottled green carpet of Irish fields, farmhouses dotting the vales like tiny boats on a deep green sea, legendary Celtic swans floating on sapphire lakes, Viking fortresses and castles belonging to ancient Irish kings. And rosy-cheeked lasses with hair of flame, running through fields of wildflowers, arms outstretched to greet their lovers.

When his uncharacteristically fanciful mind went on to imagine Claren lying in a field of poppies, the smile on her face directed at him in such a way to make him burn, Dash tried, without success, to force the provocative image back into his mutinous subconscious.

The sun had set beyond the horizon. Although it was not yet dark, dusk had turned the sky a soft, silvery blue. No longer needing the sunglasses, Dash took them off and tossed them onto the dashboard.

Claren had been wanting to see the man's eyes for the past four hours. Now that she had, she almost wished he'd kept the glasses on. They were smoky gray. Dark, intense. They were, she decided, the kind of eyes a wolf would have. His slate lashes were long and full enough to belong to a woman, but there was nothing womanly in his gaze. Her mind went blank.

"You were telling me what happened to the town," Dash reminded her after a long pause.

Directing her gaze out the windshield, Claren shrugged and pretended a sudden interest in a family of tourists coming out of the ice-cream parlor. A father, mother and two children—one boy, one girl. They were laughing, obviously enjoying the scenery, the day and each other.

The engaging sight stirred Claren's longings for a family of her own. A family she'd believed she was going to have with Elliott. She sighed.

"The deal fell through." Renewed anger toward her former fiancé added an acid edge to her voice. Clearing her throat, she struggled against her rising temper. "And the line linking Seattle and Tacoma on the east side of Puget Sound got all the traffic. The town died."

Dash, who'd been watching her carefully, took note of both her sigh and her anger. Claren O'Neill was not a simple woman. He'd do well to remember that.

"Obviously the rumors of its death were exaggerated," he said.

Although not large, the town appeared to be a thriving little center of commerce, based mainly, from what Dash could tell of the shops lining the street, on tourism. Antique shops, their windows crowded with heirlooms and undoubtedly overpriced memorabilia, stores offering new-age crystals, an amazing number of galleries catering to Northwestern art, bookstores and restaurants appeared to provide the major source of employment.

"It's a special place," Claren said simply. "The people who live here now are here because they've chosen not to be anywhere else."

Dash couldn't understand such a sentimental attraction to a place. The longest he'd ever stayed in any one place—other than his childhood, which had been spent in Guthrie, Oklahoma—was New York City. He'd managed to live in Manhattan for three long years.

The first year, he had admittedly found the city an exciting change from the historic Oklahoma frontier town he'd grown up in. But, unaccustomed to staying in one place very long, and finding the social customs so alien that he might as well be living on Jupiter, he'd come to feel like a prisoner in his Fifth Avenue apartment. He'd stayed two more years, only because his wife refused to leave.

Their relationship had continued to disintegrate until eventually both admitted that a marriage between two such dissimilar persons had been a mistake. When he'd packed his things and walked out the door for the last time, Dash had had the feeling that his wife was every bit as relieved to see him go as he was to escape.

"So where now?" he asked as he drove through what appeared to be the business district. There was only one traffic light the entire length of the street. And it was flashing.

"You can park over there," Claren pointed. "I just need to pop into a store and pick up some jeans."

Dash pulled the car up in front of a three-story red-brick building that looked as if it had once served as a warehouse. The first floor housed a women's clothing shop. The calligraphic sign on the second-floor window pronounced it to be the home of the Olympic Gallery, featuring Indian and Eskimo art.

The third floor, whose wide bank of windows offered a spectacular view of the strait, was a café, named Pelican's Roost. The fragrant charcoal aroma rising from the restaurant's smokestack reminded Dash that he hadn't eaten since breakfast.

"After you get your clothes, we'll have dinner."

Arrogant ox, Claren considered silently. "After I get my clothes, I intend to go to my uncle's house."

Rather than being irritated by her behavior, Dash liked the way Claren was constantly challenging him. Her prickly attitude was a refreshing change from the accommodating behavior he usually insisted upon from his women.

His women? Dash frowned and cut the thought off before it had time to take root. Claren O'Neill Wainwright was nothing more than his current assignment, he reminded himself firmly.

All right, perhaps she represented more than just a job. But that was only because he'd liked her uncle. Having been Darcy's friend, he felt an obligation to make certain that no harm came to the woman.

And no harm would, he vowed, not for the first time since he'd received Darcy's letter. Unless, of course, St. John was right and Claren was in on the caper that had gotten her uncle killed. In that case, the matter would be out of his hands. There would be little he could do to protect her.

Claren watched the blistering scowl move across his face and wondered at its cause. If it hadn't been for her uncle's reassuring words that she could trust Dash MacKenzie, she would have thought him dangerous. As it was, Claren had more than her share of reservations about spending any more time than necessary with the man.

"When was the last time you ate?" Dash asked.

"Why?"

Did she have to question every little thing? Dash wondered how in the hell that weak-spined Elliott Byrd had ever believed he was going to handle such a woman. That thought was followed by the unwilling idea that if he didn't wrap things up fast, those incredible sharp eyes might see through his subterfuge. It had been a long time since he'd lied for a living, and Dash didn't like discovering that he was out of practice.

"Because, as an accomplice to your rather dramatic escape, I feel responsible for you," he said. "And I'm damned if I'm going to have you fainting from hunger."

"I never faint."

"There's always a first time." Reaching out, he cupped her chin. "You know, if you keep sticking that chin out like that, Irish, some day someone's going to take you up on the challenge and pop you one."

"Someone like you?"

Dash decided that hauteur suited her every bit as well as her temper. There was no fear in those green eyes, rather a cool, maddening disdain.

"Don't tempt me." Unable to resist, he stroked his thumb along her jawline. His eyes brushed over her mouth, and in that brief moment, Dash knew that, as dangerous an act as it would be, before this was over he was going to taste those full, pouting lips.

"Don't touch me like that."

"How would you like me to touch you?"

He smiled, allowing his gaze to roam her tense body with a masculine insolence that she suspected was inherent. As she watched the heat rise in those smoky eyes, Claren felt a quick, breathless pressure in her chest. *No*, she warned herself. *Not now. And especially not him.*

She'd barely escaped one disastrous relationship. Getting involved in yet another the very same day would be the height of folly. Like jumping out of the frying pan right into the fire. Some deep-seated feminine instinct told Claren that this man could make the flames very hot indeed.

"Mr. MacKenzie—"

"It's Dash." He had watched the awareness rise in her eyes and damned himself for encouraging an involvement he couldn't afford.

Claren ignored his murmured correction. "Mr. MacKenzie," she repeated firmly, "just because you happened to come along at a convenient time and gave me a ride doesn't mean you have any business telling me what to do."

"I don't know," Dash countered. "Haven't you ever heard that old proverb about once you save a life, it's yours?"

"I'd hardly call driving a person to the ferry saving a life."

"You're right. I could have just left you out on the road and let your fiancé and your relatives catch up with you."

She'd never thought of that. Claren wondered if Elliott would run after her. No, she decided, he never would have risked getting his cutaway sweaty. Aunt Winifred undoubtedly had taken to her bed with one of her convenient migraines, leaving the embarrassing explanations to her long-suffering husband.

"Well, as much as I appreciate your help, I'm perfectly capable of taking care of myself from now on."

"The light'll be gone soon. Don't tell me you intend to walk all the way to Darcy's house in the dark?"

Having already considered that, Claren was ready for him. "Anyone in town would be more than happy to give me a ride."

From what Darcy had told him about Port Vancouver, Dash decided that was undoubtedly true. Frustrated, but not accustomed to letting a woman win the upper hand, he tried another tack. "So you really don't want to eat with me?"

He was up to something. A wicked gleam had turned his eyes to silver, allowing Claren to realize exactly how Red Riding Hood must have felt facing down the Big Bad Wolf.

She crossed her arms; her back was pressed against the passenger door. "No."

"Don't tell me you're afraid?"

"Afraid?" Angry insults rose in her throat; years of reining in her tumultuous nature had her swallowing them. But just barely. "You overestimate yourself, MacKenzie."

"Perhaps." Leaving the car, he went around and opened her passenger door. "Perhaps not." The fire he saw in her eyes rivaled that in her hair. For not the first time in the past four hours, Dash found himself admiring both.

"You'd better get to your shopping," he suggested. "Before the store closes."

With an inarticulate murmur that could have meant anything, Claren gathered up her skirts and left the car in a furious rustle of satin. But not before Dash had been treated to an appealing expanse of slender leg, clad in sheer ivory hose.

"Do you need any money?"

Was he actually offering to buy clothing for a woman he'd just met? What kind of man was Dash MacKenzie? If only Darcy were alive, he could answer that question. But if her uncle were alive, this frustrating, dangerously attractive man wouldn't have come to Washington in the first place.

"Fortunately I have all my credit cards," she said, reaching back into the car to retrieve her bag. "They'll do until I can have my bank transfer my account to the local bank."

"So you're really going to stay."

He'd already decided she had spunk. But as the ferry had made its way across the sound, taking her farther and farther away from the comfortable life she'd known, the secure, privileged world she'd grown accustomed to, Dash couldn't help wondering if she'd changed her mind.

After all, he couldn't deny that she had built a rather enviable life in Seattle. If a person were interested in a successful conventional existence. Personally Dash had found such a life-style stifling.

"Yes, I am." Having acted on impulse, Claren had half expected to suffer doubts. But the nearer they'd gotten to Port Vancouver, the more she was convinced that she'd made the right decision.

"What about Darcy's condition?"

When the attorney had first read her Darcy's will, Claren had been stunned by her uncle's autocratic demand that if she wanted to inherit his home, she would have to give up her thriving professional career, move into the house and devote one year to perfecting her talent. Now, given all that had happened in the past few hours, she realized that in his own way Darcy had been providing her with an escape route.

"I still think my uncle was overly optimistic about my talent," she admitted.

A successful artist himself, Darcy had spent the major part of each of his visits trying to teach Claren to paint. And although she'd steadfastly demonstrated scant talent, he'd been convinced that her stiffly proper upbringing was simply damming up her inspiration.

"But I'm willing to give it the old college try," she said with a renewed burst of determination, "if it means keeping the house."

Her earlier irritation with Dash was forgotten as she found herself looking forward to the next twelve months. "I truly love that house," she said with a soft smile that pulled at Dash.

He felt himself softening and steeled against it. He refused to fall prey to emotions he'd successfully blocked for years. Besides, things could get extremely dirty and dangerous before this was over. He wouldn't be very much help if he allowed himself to become pre-occupied with this attraction that neither of them wanted.

"Well, you have that much in common with your uncle." Dash was struck with a sudden, irrational urge to run the back of his hand up her cheek. Plunging his fists into the pocket of his jeans, he said, "Have fun shopping. I'll go upstairs and get us a table."

"Perhaps I haven't made myself clear. I am not eating dinner with you."

"Fine. You can sit and watch me eat."

Something in her was softening. She tilted her head, as if to study him from a new angle. "You're a very frustrating man."

"So I've been told."

The hell with it. Giving in to temptation, as he'd feared all along he would, he allowed his hand to trail up the side of her face. Her skin was as soft as the underside of the hibiscus blossoms that had bloomed in Jamaica. As his fingers stroked their way from her jawline to her temple, the color that bloomed in her cheeks rivaled the crimson hue of those very same tropical flowers.

The intimate touch caused her nerves to hum. A band of tension settled along her shoulders. "Would you please stop touching me?"

"No," he said pleasantly. "I don't think I will. Anyone ever tell you that you're very touchable, Irish?"

It was time to be firm, Claren told herself. Very firm.

"Really, MacKenzie, if you don't keep your hands off me—"

"I know," he murmured, intrigued by the touch, the scent of her skin. "The judo." God help him, he wanted more. Much, much more. "I'll find myself lying on my back in the gutter."

The old-fashioned gas streetlight behind him flickered on, casting his face in harsh relief. Claren felt as if her feet were nailed to the sidewalk. She reached up to brush his seductive touch away, but instead found her hand suddenly held captive in his much larger one.

His hand, she noted irrelevantly, was strong. The row of calluses she felt at the base of his fingers suggested that he was a man who was not afraid of hard physical work.

Their eyes met. And then their minds.

Did those turbulent thoughts belong to him? she wondered, dazed by the storm raging inside her. Or were they hers? Either way, they held her absolutely spellbound.

The sky overhead was a darkening purple, studded with weak, stuttering early stars. But it was crystal clear, without a sign of a cloud. So where had the lightning come from? Dash wondered. And why was he hearing thunder?

This wasn't what he'd planned. It wasn't what he wanted. Dash knew that if he didn't back away now, he'd be lost.

Too late. "You're going to have dinner with me," he heard himself saying.

It was not a question. Even as Claren told herself she should be irritated by his arrogant belief that he could make a woman jump through hoops for him, she found the lingering heat in his stormy gray eyes impossible to resist.

They were both shaken and both equally determined not to show it. The whistle of the ferry, leaving the Port Vancouver terminal on its way across Discovery Bay, hung on the early-evening air. Neither Claren nor Dash paid any attention to it. The raucous cries of the sea gulls, following in the ferry's wake in search of fish, also went unnoticed. Claren only heard the wild pounding of her heart; Dash's ears were still reverberating from that out-of-the-blue thunderclap.

"I suppose I have to eat," she said with a calm that belied the turmoil battering away inside her.

Dash felt a surge of relief and chose to ignore it. "Good. How's the food upstairs?" He was still holding her hand. When his thumb brushed against the inside of her wrist, he felt the quick, surprised increase of her pulse.

"It's very good," she heard herself say. Her voice sounded far away, as if it was coming from the bottom of the sea. "If you like seafood."

"Seafood's fine." Slowly, reluctantly he released her hand. He found himself not wanting to let her go. Not yet. "There's one more thing."

She definitely didn't trust the gleam in his smoky eyes. "What?"

"Why are you afraid to call me Dash?"

Because it's too personal, Claren admitted. "I told you," she insisted, "I'm not afraid of you."

"Aren't you?" He took a step closer and cupped the back of her neck with his hand. "I have another name besides MacKenzie. Think you could try using it?"

She took a moment to answer. "I'll think about it."

"That's all I can ask," he said agreeably. Only the tensing of his fingers on her neck revealed his annoyance. "Want some company while you shop?"

No! The idea of taking off her clothes, knowing that this man was waiting right outside the dressing room, was more of a risk than Claren was prepared to take.

"No, thank you," she said politely.

He wanted to leave. He wanted never to leave. Damn. What he wanted, Dash realized with a great deal of trepidation, was to spend the rest of his life just looking at her. Darcy had been right after all, he decided. The woman was beautiful. It was with a great deal of reluctance that he released her.

"I'll be waiting upstairs, then."

"Fine." Why was it that her feet refused to obey her command to move? "I'll see you later."

"Later."

He leaned against the car and watched her enter the store. It was obvious that she was well known; both silver-haired clerks came rushing up to her. From what he could tell through the display windows, her wedding dress was causing quite a stir.

The women began racing around the store, plucking clothing off racks. All the while, Dash noted, she kept talking, her graceful hands emphasizing her words.

Inside the shop, Claren regarded the owners with amused fondness. She had known Mildred and Maxine Browne for years. Twin sisters, forty-five years ago they'd married Port Vancouver's other pair of twins, John and Robert Browne. For all those years, they had lived next door to each other, worn their hair the same way and dressed in similar clothing, although Mildred favored navy blue, brown and olive green, while her sister, displaying an independent flair, usually chose scarlet.

Three summers ago Robert Browne had died of a heart attack, leaving Maxine a widow. Which is when she began pursuing Darcy with a single-mindedness the sixty-three-year-old Irish bachelor found absolutely terrifying. The thought of her uncle, whom she'd always regarded as invincible, being afraid of a tiny, ninety-pound widow had amused Claren at the time.

The sisters fluttered about her like eager birds, gathering up clothing from all corners of the room, Mildred plucking earth tones from the racks, Maxine diving into a new arrival of fluorescent sweaters.

"You did the right thing, dear," Maxine said as she handed Claren a sunshine yellow sweatshirt. A pair of puffins sitting atop a rock had been embossed on the front of the shirt.

"Absolutely," Mildred agreed, adding a pair of slim gray linen slacks and matching cotton blouse to the pile.

"You know, dear," Maxine confided, fluffing her cotton candy silver hair, "although neither one of us ever wanted to say anything—"

"For fear of hurting your feelings," Mildred broke in.

"Sister," Maxine complained, "I was talking."

"I realize that, Sister," Mildred agreed calmly. "But I felt it important that Claren realize that we were only thinking of her."

"Of course we were. And that's precisely why we should have spoken up in the first place," Maxine insisted. "Which is what I've been saying from the very beginning."

It was obviously a sore point. Claren watched Mildred's spine stiffen, as if someone had slipped a rod of cold steel down the back of her brown-and-black-checked dress.

"Well, it doesn't matter any longer," Mildred pointed out haughtily. "Since Claren came to her senses on her own. As I always said she would." The older woman patted Claren's arm. "I knew you were an intelligent woman, dear. I had faith in your judgment."

Realizing that her impending marriage had been the subject of a great deal of local conjecture, Claren managed a murmured "Thank you."

"You know, dear," Mildred said, "that Byrd fellow was never right for you."

"We were both concerned that he wasn't man enough to make you a proper husband," Maxine blurted out. She arched a silver brow. "Personally I always thought he was a bit of a sissy, if you get my drift."

"Sister!" An expression of absolute shock crossed Mildred's furrowed face. "Remember your manners. Don't you recall Mother teaching us that there are some subjects that shouldn't be discussed in polite company?"

She shook her gray head as she turned back to Claren. "Please, dear, don't pay any attention to Maxine. Ever since she started watching that Oprah Winfrey television program, my sister's conversation has become increasingly scandalous."

"It's important to know what's going on in the world," Maxine shot back. "Unlike some of us, who are more than content living in the past." Undaunted by her sister's censure, Maxine gave Claren a warm, reassuring smile. "Everyone in town agreed with me about Elliott, but don't worry, dear. The right man will come along one of these days. And when he does, you'll know it."

Claren returned the older woman's smile, not wanting to get into an argument about Elliott's manhood, or lack of it. She knew that as wives of lumbermen, Mildred and Maxine Browne had their own definition of masculine. And in their dictionary, a suit-clad stockbroker just didn't qualify.

"Thank you for the encouragement," she said. "But believe me, after today I'm in no hurry to get involved with any man."

"That's what we always said when we were girls," Maxine agreed knowingly. "Until we met our own Mr. Rights."

"Or, in our case, our Mr. Brownes," Mildred said.

Claren shook her head "Well, the way I feel right now, if Mr. Right did suddenly show up, I'd turn and run the other way."

That was when she made the mistake of looking out the window. Instead of having gone upstairs to the restaurant, Dash was still standing on the sidewalk, leaning against the fender of the car with his arms crossed, watching her.

Their eyes met only for a brief instant, but in that fleeting moment, Claren knew that her life had inexplicably changed.

Was it possible to fall in love in an instant? Claren had never believed in such a romantic notion. Now she realized she might well have been wrong.

The timing was impossible. After all, this was to have been her wedding day. The day of her marriage to another man. Claren decided that only a very flighty woman would leave her groom at the altar and fall in love with a total stranger the very same day.

A very flighty woman indeed, Claren told herself.

Or a black sheep.

Although she'd spent half her life in the United States, trying to behave in a way that would help her fit into her aunt's stodgy, socially disapproving set, Claren was still Irish enough to believe in fate. And destiny.

4

DESIRE MADE HIM EDGY.

Dash sat at a table in the far corner of the Pelican's Roost, impatiently nursing a drink, waiting for Claren's arrival. How long did it take a woman to buy a few clothes? Remembering his former wife's extended shopping sprees in Paris, London and Manhattan, he decided that he could well spend the rest of the night in this chair.

The restaurant was reminiscent of Port Vancouver's seagoing days. The walls were paneled in pine that had been stained to a light blue-gray, designed to appear that the pine had been weathered by decades of wind and water.

A mural of an ancient whaling expedition covered one wall; on the others were antique signs, two of which read Ladies Present, Watch Your Language, and First Fight, Last Fight, Barred For Life. Over the arched doorway, a carved wooden bust—a female figurehead of Rubenesque proportions, salvaged from the prow of an ancient galleon—stood eternal guard.

The table had been left bare, displaying a rich antique wood that glowed with the patina of time. The lighting was soft, flickering in the shadowy corners. In the center of the table, adding illumination without brightness, a white candle glowed in a brass seaman's lantern. As he scanned the handwritten menu, Dash saw that the wealth of seafood continued the nautical theme.

Dash ordered another drink and decided that if Claren didn't show up soon, he'd go ahead and order the fried-oyster appetizer. He'd no sooner gotten irritated about her lack of punctuality than another thought occurred to him. One that sent ice up his spine. Perhaps something had happened to her.

That was ridiculous. After all, she was only two flights down the stairs. Remembering how steep and narrow and dark those stairs had been, Dash pushed away from the table, cursing himself for letting down his guard like some damn amateur. Although he'd begun to suspect that St. John was wrong about Claren O'Neill Wainwright's involvement in her uncle's dangerous scheme, the fact remained that she was the only lead to the missing treasure. And if he could track her down this easily, others could, too.

He'd just gotten to his feet when he saw her, standing in the doorway beside a brightly colored poster announcing the Hot Jazz and Cool Blues music festival. Her arms were filled with shopping bags. Relief was instantaneous.

Claren's eyes swept the restaurant slowly, adjusting to the dim light. Then she saw him. The feeling that flooded over her was reminiscent of the feeling she'd experienced when she'd seen him standing outside the store window, watching her. But this time it was stronger. Much, much stronger.

Forcing down her nervousness, Claren handed her packages over to the hostess, exchanged a few words, then walked across the room to join him.

Eschewing the jeans and sweaters worn by the other women in the restaurant, she was wearing a red silk dress that clung in all the right places. From the way she walked toward him, Dash knew that she was aware of garnering the attention of every male in the place. Including his.

He'd been right about her legs, Dash determined. Her skirt stopped midthigh, revealing them to be surprisingly long for a woman of her size. They were also lean and firm. Lust hit like a fist in the solar plexus.

What the hell was the matter with him? Jet lag, Dash determined, conveniently forgetting that he never got jet lag. Or flu. Manners, unused for too long, reasserted themselves just in time for Dash to remember to pull out her chair.

The unexpected act of chivalry pleased Claren, but didn't surprise her. From what she'd seen of him thus far, she'd suspected that Dash was an old-fashioned man. Having spent the past three years engaged to a modern, egocentric nineties male, she found herself intrigued by the differences she'd already discovered between the two men.

"Thank you." She smiled up at him. "I hope I didn't keep you waiting too long."

The dress, as scarlet as sin, should have clashed with her hair, but for some reason didn't. When someone at the far corner of the room called out her name, she turned and waved, causing the silk to shift enticingly over small, firm breasts.

"It was worth it."

Claren hadn't wanted to try on the dress, which was so unlike the conservative clothing she usually favored. But Maxine had insisted. That was all it had taken. Standing in front of the dressing room's three-way mirror, Claren had been stunned by both the amazing transformation in her appearance and the feminine confidence the dress inspired.

Now, surprised and pleased by the admiration in Dash's gaze, Claren was glad that she had given in to Maxine's sales pressure.

"Did you just give me a compliment?" she asked.

"I guess I did."

Claren digested that and decided that Dash was not a man to flatter lightly. What was it he'd said? That he'd known she'd be a sucker for sweet talk, flowers and candlelight. His tone, at the time, had not been approving.

"Thank you," she said.

He'd seen the quick flash of surprised pleasure flood into her eyes and was surprised that it took so little to please her. It made him wonder what kind of fool Byrd was to let this woman get away.

"I just have one question."

"What's that?"

"Did you buy it to stir up my juices? Or was it intended for the male population of Port Vancouver in general?"

His eyes had turned cool, hard and cynical. Refusing to let his rudeness get under her skin, Claren decided to pay him back for the way he had of unsettling her.

A mischievous devil perched on her silk-clad shoulder and whispered in her ear, advising her to show Dash that she was not the naive runaway bride he obviously perceived her to be, but a woman accustomed to wrapping intriguing, dangerous-looking Casanovas around her little finger.

Which, of course, was an out-and-out lie. Her scant experience with men had always been centered solely on Elliott, but Dash MacKenzie had no way of knowing that.

"Well, now that you mention it, I did buy it with you in mind." She curved her lips in a slow, seductive smile and, ignoring the interested glances from an elderly woman at a nearby table, reached out and trailed her fingernail slowly down the front of his faded blue chambray work shirt. "Is it working?"

"Move your hand a little lower, sweetheart, and you'll find out quick enough."

Their eyes held. "Are you always this purposely horrid?" Claren asked.

"Actually, I am. Are you always this beautiful?"

Prepared for another round in what appeared to be an ongoing battle of wills, Claren found herself distracted by the honest sincerity in his statement.

She lowered her hand, and her gaze, to her lap. When she finally looked up at him again, her eyes were filled with questions.

"I don't understand you."

He shrugged. "That's probably for the best."

Claren didn't think so. "That's a rather mysterious answer," she murmured. "But then you're a rather mysterious man."

She was too damn intuitive. Dash was wondering how long he'd be able to fool her when a waitress arrived at their table with his drink.

Watching the voluptuous bottle-blonde bat her thick, blatantly false lashes at Dash, Claren wondered if there was a female anywhere who could resist this man's rugged, dangerous looks. Finally getting the waitress's attention, she ordered a glass of chardonnay.

A not uncomfortable silence settled over the table. For now Dash was content to just look at her. The vivid hue of the dress enhanced her porcelain complexion. The gleaming silk looked incredibly soft; Dash suspected that her skin would be softer.

"I like that color. It suits you."

Never one to hold a grudge, Claren's quick grin lit up her eyes, rivaling the glowing candlelight. "I like it, too. Do you know it's the first bright thing I've bought in years?"

She thought of all her neat little business suits—all stark black except for one sophisticated winter wool in charcoal gray—hanging in the walk-in closet of her aunt's guest room. She'd worn them as camouflage, Claren realized now, in a desperate attempt to hide the tempestuous person living inside her calm, proper exterior. Well, that predictable, boring woman was gone. And Claren wouldn't miss her. Not even a little.

The waitress returned with her wine. Claren murmured a polite thank-you, but since every atom of the woman's attention was directed at Dash, Claren was not surprised when the waitress failed to answer.

"It's funny," she said when they were alone again, "but I think I know exactly how Superman must feel whenever he takes off his boring old Clark Kent disguise."

"Darcy always complained that you spent too much time pretending to be something you weren't."

"I wasn't pretending," Claren protested. "Not really."

He was staring into her face, studying her with that same unapologetic intensity as before. "Then what do you call it?"

"Trying to fit in, I suppose." She shrugged. "Doesn't everyone?"

"Not me."

It was Claren's turn to study him. She leaned back in the maple captain's chair and gave him a long, judicious look. No. He wouldn't. Dash MacKenzie would not bend for anyone, or anything. Instinct told her that he was a loner, a man who preferred distant and less-traveled roads. Having always been close to her uncle, she recognized the all-too-familiar wanderlust in Dash.

But where Darcy had been open and outgoing, Dash reminded Claren of the Chinese puzzle box her uncle had brought back from Beijing for her fifteenth birthday.

Dash MacKenzie would not be an easy man to know. He would not be an easy man to love. It was a good thing, Claren decided with a burst of newly discovered optimism, that she'd always loved a challenge.

Dash watched the slow, womanly smile move across Claren's lips and wondered at its cause. "What are you thinking?"

She wondered what he'd do if she told the truth and admitted that she thought she might be falling in love with him, and she decided that he'd take off running before she could finish getting the words out. That was all right. They had plenty of time. And she wasn't going anywhere. Unfortunately she couldn't say the same for him.

"I was thinking about Darcy's house," she said.

She shouldn't try to lie. Because her face gave her away, every time. Needing to determine what exactly she knew about her uncle's penchant for treasure hunting, Dash opted not to challenge her on the obvious falsehood.

"I'd like to see it," he said nonchalantly.

"That's what I was thinking. How good are you with your hands?"

His eyes skimmed over her face deliberately, a masochistic test of his control. "I can assure you, I've never had any complaints."

Deep color—the bane of all redheads—flooded into her cheeks. The flickering glow of the candlelight added heat to her hair. Once again Dash was drawn to her. Once again he warned himself away. He couldn't let his emotions fuddle his logic. For her sake. And his.

Picking up the menu the flirtatious waitress had set at her elbow, Claren buried her face in it, pretending for a long silent time to be absorbed in the choices. Time crawled at a snail's pace. Finally, when she couldn't stand the suspense any longer, she risked a glance over the top of the menu. He was still looking at her with that brooding patience she'd come to recognize.

"You really shouldn't talk to me like that," she scolded, wondering how it was that this man, with a single word, one long look, could leave her both baffled and flustered. And wanting. "By tomorrow morning it will be all over town that we're lovers."

"You started it," Dash reminded her. He ran a lazy finger down the back of her hand. "Besides, would that be so bad?"

The storm was building inside her. Dash had been right when he called her a romantic. Before she'd moved out of her apartment, hidden in the drawer of her nightstand had been a cache of romance novels, some of which had been her mother's. Claren had always enjoyed love stories. So much so, she'd been willing to stand in line outside a theater in the Seattle rain to see *Ghost*.

In fiction, falling in love so quickly was always wonderful. Thrilling. Unfortunately she was discovering that in real life it could be terrifying.

"That it would be all over town?" she asked.

"That we were lovers." He took her hand in his, linking their fingers together. "They fit," he murmured. His smile was slow and seductive. "I thought they might."

Claren stared down at their joined hands. She wasn't prepared for this. She needed time to think. To understand what was happening to her. Twelve years of planning every deed, of censuring every word, of avoiding unseemly attention and any form of confrontation had taken their toll on her. Emotions, feelings, sensations, all were flooding over her, through her, as if escaping from a ruptured dam. It was too much for one day.

Claren could have wept with relief when the waitress chose that moment to return to take their orders. "I'll have the shrimp cocktail," she said, scanning the menu, "and the clam chowder—the New England. In a bowl, not a cup. And the Caesar salad."

Her brow furrowed as she tried to decide between the salmon and the Dungeness crab. "For an entrée, I think I'll have the grilled king salmon with chanterelles," she said finally. "No, the crab. Wait." She shook her head.

"The salmon," she decided, saving the crab for another day.

To his credit, Dash didn't blink an eye at the size of her order. "No dessert?"

"Good idea. It's berry season." Claren smiled up at the waitress. "I'll look at the dessert tray with my coffee."

"I'll have the same thing the lady's having," Dash said, handing his menu to the waitress. "But the Dungeness crab instead of the salmon.

"We'll share," he told Claren after the waitress had returned to the kitchen with their order.

"You don't have to do that."

"I want to. Although I thought you said you weren't hungry."

She looked puzzled about that, as well. "I guess shopping gives me an appetite."

"Makes sense to me." Dash leaned back in his chair and gave her another of those long, probing looks. "Want to talk about it?"

He saw so much with those fathomless deep eyes. Could he possibly read her mind? Did he realize that in the span of a few short hours, she'd begun to fall in love with him? Lord, Claren considered, the first time in years she finally allowed her emotions free reign, and what did they do but run amok?

"Talk about what?" she asked cautiously.

"About why you skipped out on your wedding."

"Oh, that." She waited while their appetizers were served. "If you don't mind, I'd rather not go into the details right now." It wasn't that she was ashamed. Far from it. But she couldn't help being embarrassed by the way she'd so badly misjudged a man she'd known since adolescence.

"Sure. There is just one thing I'm curious about."

She crossed her legs with a rustle of silk. "Oh? And here I thought you were the man with all the answers."

Although he enjoyed the way she had of standing up to him, if he'd been a believer in fate, Dash would have decided that Claren O'Neill Wainwright had been born to complicate his life. Her looks, the way she moved, her scent, the way she had of continually challenging him were driving him to the brink of aggravation. And beyond, dammit, right into obsession.

"Did you love him?"

Although she wasn't familiar with the logistics of romantic triangles, Claren didn't consider it entirely appropriate to discuss the man she'd been about to marry with the man she was falling in love with. "Who?"

"Byrd."

"I thought I did."

"And now?"

"Now?"

Was she purposefully taunting him? Or was she simply incredibly obtuse? "Do you love the guy now?"

"No." She speared a jumbo shrimp. "Not at all."

"But you were going to marry him," he probed.

"I was going to marry him." Claren put down her shrimp fork with an air of obvious frustration. "The definitive word is *was*. Elliott Byrd and I are past tense. Finished. Kaput. Over."

The waitress removed the shrimp bowls and replaced them with the chowder.

"So what changed your mind?"

Picking up her glass, Claren took a sip of wine. The last thing she wanted to do was talk about Elliott. She wanted to know more about Dash MacKenzie.

"You never were very specific about what you did for a living," she said. "Are you sure you've never been a policeman?"

Dash was surprised and annoyed at her sudden change in subject. "No. Why?"

"I suppose it's the way you have of looking at me," she decided. She stirred her chowder, her mind on Dash's question. "Rather like a G-man giving the mobster the third degree in all those 'Untouchables' reruns they show on cable twenty-four hours a day." When he wasn't looking at her as if he was about to take her to bed, she tacked on mentally.

It took an effort, but Dash managed to keep his expression bland and his fingers from tensing on his glass. "Are you a mobster?"

"No." She gave him a direct, level look. "Are you a G-man?"

"No." It was true. So far as it went.

"Then what do you do?"

"I told you—"

"I know," she broke in with a frustrated huff. Attempting to learn about this man was like trying to become better acquainted with the Sphinx. "A little of this, a little of that." The salad was next. Dash wondered where she intended to put it all. If she ate like this on a regular basis, he was surprised she wasn't the size of the Goodyear blimp.

"That's about it," Dash said agreeably.

Claren contemplated dumping her salad right into his lap. She tried again. "What are your plans?"

"Immediate or long-term?"

Even as he dodged her question, Claren admitted she deserved it. Hadn't she done the same thing to him? "Immediate."

She'd already seen the restlessness in him. A deep-seated restlessness her uncle had shared, in spades. A man like this would never stay in one place very long, Claren warned herself.

Dash shrugged with feigned nonchalance. "This is a nice part of the country," he said. "Now that I've come all this way, I may as well stick around and do some sight-seeing."

If Claren had been disturbed by her feelings for Dash, she was appalled at the relief she felt. "The fishing's great this time of year. And, of course, some of the best hiking trails in the country are in the Olympic National Forest."

"So I've heard."

Another thought occurred to her. "Do you have a place to stay?"

"No. But I saw some motels, along with a couple of bed-and-breakfast places while we were driving through town. I figure I can crash at one of them for a few days."

"They're very nice," she assured him. "But some of them are rather expensive."

He was about to assure her that price wouldn't be a problem when it occurred to him that she was on the verge of handing him the key to Darcy's house. So he kept his mouth shut and waited. It didn't take long.

Claren had seen the frown shadow his face when she mentioned price. Heaven knows, traveling was always expensive, and from the well-worn appearance of his clothing, she concluded that unlike her uncle Darcy, whose paintings had commanded an astronomical price, Dash was far from a wealthy man. She suddenly realized that she hadn't bothered to reimburse him for the cost of the plane flight from Jamaica to Seattle. Reaching into the oversize tote she'd hung over the back of the chair, Claren pulled out her checkbook.

"MacKenzie," she murmured, "is that with an *M-a-c* or an *M-c?*"

"*M-a-c.* What do you think you're doing?"

"I'm reimbursing you for your airline ticket."

"What?"

It was obvious that he wasn't rich. It was even more obvious that he had a right to his pride. Chastising herself for not being more diplomatic, Claren said, "Mr. MacKenzie—Dash—it was very thoughtful of you to come all this way just to bring me Darcy's photo album. But as you pointed out earlier, I have a very comfortable life. I can certainly afford to pay you back."

It was one thing to spy on her. That, Dash had told himself over and over again since leaving Jamaica, was strictly business. But he was damned if he was going to take her money.

"That isn't necessary."

"But—"

He plucked the checkbook out of her hand and tossed it back into the tote. "I said I can handle the plane fare. Besides, I was getting tired of the islands. This will be a nice change."

His words underscored Claren's feeling that he was not the type of man to settle down. Any woman foolish enough to fall in love with Dash MacKenzie should not expect a happily-ever-after.

"I had a thought earlier," Claren said as if she were walking on eggshells. "And if you won't be offended, I'd like to make you an offer."

"What kind of offer?"

"Well, Darcy isn't the tidiest person in the world. And he does tend to get distracted planning his treasure hunts."

It did not escape Dash's notice that Claren used the present tense. His first thought was that Darcy's death still hadn't completely sunk in. His second, and less palatable thought, was that perhaps she knew something that Dash didn't. Like the fact that Darcy had faked his death in order to pull off the heist of the decade. That would explain why the divers hadn't found his body.

Although he still hated to accept St. John's theory about Darcy having been part of an international terrorist cell, Dash had to admit that it wasn't totally inconceivable that the old man may have been tempted by a boatload of smuggled booty.

"Your uncle did have a serious case of treasure fever," Dash agreed. He remembered Darcy saying that the sight of the ocean floor carpeted with gold coins was something no man could ever forget.

"He dreamed of finding a galleon like the *Santa Margarita*," she said, naming a Spanish treasure galleon that had gone down off the Florida Keys during a hurricane in 1622.

"I remember when the *Santa Margarita* was discovered by divers in early 1980, she yielded more than twenty million dollars worth of gold, silver and artifacts," Dash said.

"But it was never just the gold my uncle was after," Claren insisted. "Darcy believed that the real treasure was the knowledge that can be gained from shipwrecks. The logs tell more than merely what cargo was on board—they give insights into cultural aspects of the time. Why, Darcy said that the *Pandora*, the ship that was sent to bring back the Bounty mutineers, was the most important wreck in the Southern Hemisphere, because of its historical significance and the fact that it was—"

"A virtual storehouse of navy life in the eighteenth century," Dash interjected dryly.

"You've heard the story."

"Several times."

"Then you'll understand that my uncle's interests were always far-reaching."

That was precisely what St. John believed. Dash was concerned that although Claren certainly didn't appear to be a thief or smuggler, experience had taught him that appearances could be deceiving.

"You were about to make me an offer," Dash reminded her brusquely.

"Oh. That's right."

Claren dragged her mind back to her original train of thought. What was wrong with her today? She was normally a very decisive, organized person. She always planned every aspect of her life in detail, and her mind never went careening off in all different directions, as it seemed to do whenever she attempted to converse with Dash.

"Yes. Well, as I was saying, Darcy wasn't very neat. And he wasn't ever in the state long enough to oversee the normal type of everyday repairs a house involves.

So I was thinking, since you seem to be out of work right now, and the house is in dire need of immediate help and you said that you were good with your hands—"

"I said I'd never received any complaints," Dash corrected.

Once again that soft blush colored her cheeks. "Anyway," she continued, pretending not to be moved by the devil in his eyes, "I thought that if you were any good at carpentry work, perhaps you'd like a job."

"A job?"

Claren couldn't miss the disbelief in his tone and worried that she'd managed to insult him, after all. "Well, of course, it was only a suggestion. But it would come with room and board, and since you're currently out of—uh, between jobs," she corrected quickly, "and with the jazz festival in town this weekend, you'll never find a place to stay, so I thought it might solve both our problems."

Dash had been afraid that he was going to have to live out of his car to keep an eye on Darcy's niece. Instead, the woman had fallen into his lap like a ripe plum.

"It just might at that." He rubbed his chin thoughtfully, appearing to take time to ponder her offer. "All right," he declared, "you've got yourself a handyman."

Claren let out a breath she'd been unaware of holding. "About your fee—"

"Let's worry about that later." The thought of accepting money from her bothered him more than the deception. At her worried look, he said, "I'd hate to ruin this excellent dinner with a financial discussion."

They finished the meal in companionable silence. There was more that needed to be said, emotions that needed to be dealt with, but there would be time for all that later. For now it was enough to enjoy the moment, Dash decided.

Because before this was over, circumstances would force them to face a reality that promised to be anything but pleasant.

5

THE FOG HAD COME IN, wrapping the town in a soft silver blanket. As they drove to the house, located ten miles outside Port Vancouver, the car's headlights cut a yellow swath through the darkness.

"I'll never be able to eat again," Claren moaned.

"You should have skipped the blackberries and cream. Do you always eat like a starved orphan?" The inappropriateness of that particular question sounded like a brass gong.

"I'm sorry." Dash shook his head, disgusted by his behavior. "That was an incredibly insensitive thing to say."

"Is that an apology?" From what she'd seen thus far, Claren decided that Dash was not a man accustomed to asking for forgiveness.

"I suppose it is."

Claren smiled. "Then I accept. And as for the blackberries, fresh fruit is one of the perks of living in Washington. Besides, I couldn't resist the temptation."

"Have trouble with temptation, do you, Irish?"

"Always," she said with a soft, rippling sigh. "Poor Aunt Winifred. I think I was the bane of her existence. 'Watch and pray,'" Claren quoted, "'that ye enter not into temptation.' Matthew 26:41." Considering the sexual chemistry that kept flashing between them, she wasn't about to continue the quote about the spirit being willing, but the flesh weak.

"Very good," Dash said, fighting down the surge of angry memory her words created. His back still bore the faint crisscrossing of scars inflicted in childhood by a hell-and-brimstone minister. "You must have gotten all the gold stars in Sunday school."

"Aunt Winifred was fond of quoting scripture." Another sigh. "I think she had an appropriate quote for everything."

"You should have told her that you could resist everything except temptation," Dash suggested.

A handyman who could quote Oscar Wilde. Once again Claren was intrigued by the complexities of this man. And although she had hundreds of questions, she'd have to be patient. Dash was not a man to open up easily. A woman would not get inside his head unless invited.

"Oh, I couldn't have done that," she insisted, returning her mind to the conversation at hand. "My aunt didn't like people who talked back to her."

"And it was important that she like you?"

From what Darcy had told him about Winifred Wainwright Palmer, the fact that she might like a person wasn't exactly proof of a sterling character. Claren's aunt was a relentless social climber; as such, she would approve of anything or anyone who could possibly improve her status in the community.

"Of course it was." Claren shifted on the seat, turning toward him, tucking her legs under her. "You have to understand," she said earnestly, "when I came to America, I was only twelve years old. I'd lost everything. My parents, my home, my country. I could tell right away that I was a terrible disappointment to my father's family.

"I didn't dress correctly, I didn't talk correctly and I didn't behave correctly. I think I realized from the very first that whatever I did would never be quite good enough."

But that hadn't stopped her from trying, Claren considered. From doing everything she thought would help her become a person her aunt and uncle could admire. And love.

"I don't believe that," Dash said. "Oh, not the part about you losing everything," he said when he felt her about to argue. "I'm talking about you not being good enough to meet your aunt's lofty standards. Although I've never met the woman, your aunt Winifred sounds like a damn fool."

She smiled. "Thank you. You've no idea how badly I need to hear that. Especially after..."

Her voice drifted off. Just thinking about her aunt's reaction to her calling off the wedding made her weary. Proclaiming that boys will be boys, her aunt had insisted Claren overlook her fiancé's little peccadillo.

Unfortunately that was exactly the problem. Elliott Byrd was a boy. A spoiled, selfish, conceited, egocentric brat.

"That must have been some fight," Dash's voice broke into her furious thoughts.

"What?"

"Your fight with that Byrd fellow. It must have been a doozie."

"What makes you say that?"

"Because it's obvious from the way your conversation dropped off that you're thinking about having run out on the wedding, and the temperature in this car just dropped at least twenty degrees."

"One of these days I'll tell you what happened," she said, not wanting any secrets between them. "But not now. I still need some time to look at it objectively."

If it didn't have anything to do with the case, Dash wasn't certain he wanted to know. He'd already gotten too close to this woman; he damn well didn't want to start sharing intimate stories.

"Whatever you say," he said agreeably. "And for the record, if you're really serious about this new outlook on life, you should quit worrying about how to make people like you. It isn't necessary."

His words were the same ones that Darcy had been telling her for a very long time. And there was a warmth underlying his tone that she hadn't heard before.

"What a nice thing to say. Does that mean that you like me?"

It was definitely a loaded question. "You're awfully stubborn."

"I know. It's an O'Neill family trait," she admitted. "One I share with my uncle. But Darcy always told me that I should think of it as tenacity."

Although it was an unpalatable thought, Dash couldn't help wondering what else she shared with her uncle. A boatload of smuggled gems, for instance?

"And you've got one hell of a temper," he said.

She grinned at that. "I know. I'm still rather amazed to discover how quickly it came back after all these years. But you're dodging the question. Do you like me?"

So many lies, Dash considered. Although he'd probably regret it, he decided to tell her what little truth he could. "Yeah, Irish," he said. "I like you. Okay?"

She folded her arms across her chest, hugging in that encouraging thought. "Okay."

They stopped at a convenience store, picking up some milk, coffee and English muffins for breakfast. Unable to resist the lure of local produce, Claren also selected cherries, blackberries and peaches, along with a selection of homemade jams and jellies. When she returned to the front of the store, where Dash was waiting, he arched a brow at her overloaded basket.

"What, no boysenberry pie?"

Claren flashed him a bright smile of gratitude. "Good idea," she said, selecting a fresh-baked pie from the glass case. "Do you want to get the ice cream, or shall I?"

Muttering something about metabolism, Dash made his way through the narrow aisles back to the frozen-foods case. When he returned, he couldn't help noticing that the teenage night clerk was looking at Claren in a way that was anything but businesslike. The kid's eyes, behind the thick lenses of his glasses, were practically burning a hole through the red silk draping Claren's pert breasts.

"Anything else, dear?" Dash asked, putting an arm around Claren's shoulders and pulling her close. "Perhaps some fresh strawberries for breakfast tomorrow morning?"

Startled by his sudden display of intimacy and the way his gray eyes had turned dark and dangerous—like those of a wolf guarding his lair—Claren could only stare and sputter an inarticulate reply.

She found her voice once they were back in the car. "Why did you do that?"

"Do what?"

"You practically stamped a No Trespassing sign on the front of my chest."

"At least it was right where the clerk would see it," Dash returned hotly. "Or didn't you notice that the horny little bastard was practically staring right through that damned dress."

Was the man actually jealous? Claren found the idea definitely appealing. "Actually I did," she said with a faint smile.

At first she'd been surprised by the young man's obvious male interest and had looked to see if there was some sexy young girl standing behind her. Then she had remembered what she was wearing and decided that Maxine was definitely right. Clothes did make the woman.

"So why didn't you tell him to paste his damn eyes somewhere else?"

"And miss watching you act like a Neanderthal?" Claren asked sweetly. "It was really quite entertaining, Dash. Why, I can't remember when I've been treated to such a primitive display of masculine possessiveness. Although I am a bit disappointed that you didn't drag me out to the car by the hair. It would have made my exit so much more dramatic."

Dash's mouth tightened, but Claren thought she saw a ghost of a smile hovering at the corner of his lips. "Next time," he muttered.

As they drove through the night, Claren recalled her parents and how they'd fallen in love. She had heard the story of her parents' courtship so many times before their death that she could recite it by heart. Many times over the past twelve lonely years, the memory of that romantic meeting had given her much-needed comfort.

Her father, James Wainwright, a Washington racehorse breeder, had come to Ireland to buy a horse at the annual Ballinasloe fair. Although the eventual price turned out to be twice what he'd planned, he'd never uttered a word of complaint about the inflated cost. Indeed, he'd gotten a bargain, James Wainwright had told his adoring daughter. Because along with the horse, he'd won the horse's owner, Claren's mother, Maura O'Neill.

That's when Claren's mother would pick up the story, explaining how she had fallen in love with the American at first sight and immediately set her cap for him.

Not that it had taken much feminine wile, James always broke in at this point, claiming that he'd tumbled head over heels for Claren's mother the first moment she'd brought the horse into the ring. After all, he'd joke with a deep rich chuckle, woman and horse were a magnificently matched set: Maura with her thick hair the very same color as King Galway's gleaming strawberry roan coat.

And although Maura's temper would always flare at this point and she would heatedly complain at being compared to a horse, from her smile and the light in her eyes when she looked at her husband, Claren understood that her mother was only pretending to be offended.

James Wainwright and Maura O'Neill were married three days later, to the delight of Maura's older brother,

Darcy, and the collective horror of James's family back in the United States. Nine months to the day of her parent's wedding, Claren was born, and for the next twelve years, there couldn't have been a happier—or more loved—girl anywhere in the world.

Dash heard Claren's soft sigh. "Tell me about the house," he said. "Darcy said it was the grandest house in America."

Claren forced away the thought of her parents' death. It had happened so many years ago, yet sometimes it seemed like only yesterday.

"Darcy's guilty of exaggeration," she answered. "As usual. But it is pretty amazing. It's situated on thirty acres, on a bluff overlooking the strait. It also has a view of Hurricane Ridge."

"Sounds nice."

"It was built in the early part of the century as a summer home for a shipping baron who'd moved to Seattle from Boston. Since the owner and his wife had eleven children, and money hadn't been a problem, the house is unusually spacious. Later it became an inn.

"That's when Darcy discovered it. He always stayed there whenever he came to Washington," Claren told Dash. "There's this one room on the third floor, with an enormous window that lets in the morning light. Darcy said that it was the best painting light in the state."

"I suppose he should have known," Dash acknowledged, thinking back on the way Darcy had toted his paints and canvas all over Jamaica, searching for the ideal spot to set up his easel.

"I suppose so," Claren agreed. "Anyway, one day about six years ago, he arrived unexpectedly and found the room booked by a pair of newlyweds. When he demanded that the owner move them to another room, the owner refused. So Darcy bought the place, right on the spot."

"That sounds like Darcy," Dash decided.

The old man was hot tempered and accustomed to having his way. For not the first time since Darcy's mysterious disappearance, Dash wondered exactly how far Darcy would go to get what he wanted. Would he actually stoop to involving his only niece? A woman who obviously adored him?

"I hope he let them finish their honeymoon before he evicted them."

Claren caught the sharp edge to his tone and glanced over at him. "Of course he did. I thought you liked Darcy."

"I do. Did," Dash corrected. "But you can't deny that he could be pretty selfish from time to time."

"True. But sometimes, perhaps being selfish is a good thing."

From her soft, thoughtful tone, Dash knew she was thinking about her habit of continually putting aside her own desires for others. "You've got a point there, Irish," he was forced to agree.

He turned off onto the private road that led to Darcy's house. They'd gone about a quarter of a mile when they were brought to a stop by a large, electronically operated wrought-iron gate.

Damn, Dash thought. St. John hadn't warned him about any gate. And he hadn't thought of it, either. After all, what did an artist need with a state-of-the-art security system? A smuggler turned terrorist, Dash considered grimly, would find such precautions more than necessary.

"What do we do now?" Although Dash knew he could get past the electronic controls with ease, he couldn't risk making Claren suspicious.

"No problem."

She unfastened her seat belt, knelt on the seat and retrieved the oversize tote from the back seat. The movement caused her dress to rise up, giving Dash an enticing view of lace-topped stockings.

Turning around, she sat back down and began digging through the bag. "Here," she said, pulling out a large silver key ring. Claren was grateful when an arched brow was Dash's only response to her carrying around the keys to a house she'd supposedly not planned to live in. "I think they're labeled."

She peered closely at the cardboard tags. Dash turned on the overhead dome light.

"Thanks." She selected one small brass key. "This is for the gate, these two operate the house alarm, and the others are for various doors and dead bolts."

The key worked. The gate opened, automatically closing behind them. A glowing full moon cut through the mist, bathing the house in a soft silver light. Eschewing the Victorian architecture of Port Vancouver, the original owner had erected a lasting tribute to his New England roots. Approaching the vast New England clapboard house with its wide wraparound porch was like time-traveling back to the days when men sailed the seas on tall-masted whaling ships, when handsome carriages with finely dressed ladies and gentlemen traversed the country lanes.

The house had been stained a light bluish gray, making it appear as if the wood had been faded by weather and time. A total of seven tall brick chimneys rose from the roof to merge with the tall clusters of Douglas firs surrounding it. Having met Darcy when the older man was living in a one-room beach bungalow, Dash was astounded by its size.

"How many rooms does this place have, anyway?" he asked as he drove up the winding stone driveway and stopped in front of the sprawling house.

"Tons," Claren said. "I've never counted them. I do remember the realtor telling Uncle Darcy that there were separate bedrooms for each of the children, and their nannies, along with a requisite number of guest rooms for visitors from Seattle. In those days it was quite a trip."

Dash had been hoping for something a little less sprawling. Searching every nook and cranny in this place could take a very long time. When Dash viewed the state-of-the-art security system Darcy had installed, he felt his heart sink.

He'd been hoping, against all appearances, that Darcy O'Neill was the innocent painter-cum-treasure-hunter he'd allegedly been. Unfortunately things were looking worse by the minute. The only question now was whether Darcy's niece was on the level.

Dash had made the mistake of trusting a female before, a television anchorwoman with incredible dark eyes that he'd bedded in Moscow. Unfortunately the woman had been using him, as he himself had used so many others over the years. It certainly hadn't been his first close call, but it had taught him an important lesson. He still carried the scar to remind him that sometimes it was the most beautiful, innocent-looking woman who could turn out to be the most deadly.

Claren located the keys to both the door and the alarm, allowing them to enter the house. The spectacular two-story entry hall was adorned with gleaming hardwood floors and was flanked by curving dual staircases. The finials on the staircases and the high ceiling moldings had been hand carved from Honduran mahogany.

"The bedrooms are all upstairs," she said. "On this floor there's a solarium garden room, several powder rooms, a dining room, the formal parlor and various smaller sitting rooms, a music room, a ballroom, a library and a remodeled, modern kitchen. Oh, and a media room."

"I thought Darcy hated television." Dash was beginning to wonder if he'd known anything about Darcy O'Neill. Dash had thought he'd experienced wealth. But he'd never, in his wildest fantasies, imagined such baronial splendor.

"Oh, he does. But he loves watching videotapes of his various expeditions."

Noting once again that she'd referred to her uncle in the present tense, Dash followed Claren down the hall into the kitchen. "Fortunately I never got around to having the electricity turned off," she said as she began putting the groceries into the vast refrigerator.

From the way Darcy had talked about his niece, Dash knew that Claren was definitely not a slacker. Nor was she one to procrastinate. Although her uncle had been extremely vocal about his disapproval of her chosen career, he'd admitted that she was brilliant at her job. And Dash knew that running a hotel, especially a five-diamond one like a Whitfield Palace Hotel, required the same attention to detail employed by the Joint Chiefs of Staff in planning an invasion.

"Perhaps you didn't get around to it because deep down you had no real intention of selling the house."

She leaned against the black glass of the refrigerator door, popped a berry into her mouth and considered his suggestion. "You know," she said, "as much as I hate to give you any credit for sensitivity, after that outrageous display in the 7-Eleven, I do believe you may be right."

"You sound surprised. Don't you think I can be sensitive to a woman's feelings when the occasion calls for it?"

Claren gave him a long look. "Honestly," she admitted finally, "I still haven't decided what I think of you."

"Yes, you have," Dash corrected, coming to stand in front of her. When his fingers brushed against her neck, Claren felt both strength and tenderness in the intimate gesture. "What you haven't decided is what you're going to do about the way you feel."

He was incredibly arrogant. But so, so right. She was drawn to him, frighteningly so. But she also still harbored enough common sense to realize that an affair with this man, no matter how brief, would leave her changed in ways she could not even begin to predict.

"You're a tough man to figure," she said.

"Not that tough. I'm simply a realist, Irish."

Claren smiled at that. "I don't think there's a single simple thing about you." She dragged her hands through her hair. "However, this is no time to dwell on it. I've had a very long and very strange day, and if you don't mind, I'm going to go to bed."

Brushing past him, she left the kitchen, using the back servant's stairs to reach the second-floor bedrooms, all too aware of Dash following close behind her.

"You can have the Cascade Room," she said, gesturing toward a door on the left side of the hall. "It has a mountain view. Unless you'd rather have a view of the strait."

"Mountains are fine. Where are you going to sleep?"

"I thought I'd take the Snoqualmie Room," she said. "It's across the hall."

No connecting door. Dash told himself it was all for the best. "Not exactly how you thought you'd be spending your wedding night, is it, Irish?"

She tried a smile that failed miserably. "No," she admitted, "it most definitely isn't. But, as Scarlett said, tomorrow is another day."

Dash found himself admiring the way she had of rallying against adversity. Darcy had said Claren had spunk. Once again Darcy was right.

"If we were living back in Scarlett's day, I would have called Byrd out for you," he said. "It would have been a duty I think I'd have enjoyed. Immensely."

"A duel." Claren's eyes lit up with enthusiasm. "What a marvelous idea. But why would it be your duty? After all, we've only just met."

"Did Byrd hurt you?"

"Yes."

"Then it would be my duty. As a man, and your protector."

She arched a russet brow. "Protector?"

"Darcy's dead. Someone has to take care of you."

Claren noticed he was no longer talking in the past tense. "I appreciate that, Dash," she said softly. "But I think I'd prefer to take care of myself. In fact," she considered brightly, "it is too bad we're living in civilized times because the more I think about it, the more I believe I would have enjoyed having a duel over my honor. But I would have wanted to be the one meeting Elliott on the green at dawn."

"Pistols or swords?"

"Pistols." Claren smiled. "They're swifter. And undoubtedly tidier."

The funny thing was, Dash considered later as he lay in the oversize bed and contemplated the plaster swirls on the ceiling, if times were different, Claren probably would have insisted on calling Byrd out for whatever sin he'd committed against her.

The idea, as outrageous as it was, made him smile.

THE SOFT CREAK of the door across the hall woke Dash instantly. Always a light sleeper, he was even more so when he was working. On more than one occasion, including that near-fatal mistake in Moscow, his life had depended on his ability to become immediately alert.

Claren jumped when he flung open the door. "I'm sorry," she gasped, staring at the deadly-looking pistol in his hand. "I didn't mean to wake you."

Watching her gather the edges of the emerald-green silk robe together, Dash knew he'd blown it. He slowly lowered the Browning automatic to his side. She was staring at the pistol as if she'd never seen a gun before.

"What kind of a handyman wakes up waving a gun?"

"I wasn't waving it."

"No," she agreed, "you weren't. You were pointing it. Directly at me."

"I wouldn't have pulled the trigger."

His casual tone concerning such an uncasual situation grated on her nerves. "You've no idea how relieved I am to hear that," she said dryly. "But that still doesn't explain what you were doing in my house," she pointed out, "with a gun." She glared down at the steel pistol in his hand. "I don't like guns. They're dangerous. And ugly."

"Ugly is in the eye of the beholder. As for dangerous, crossing the street can be dangerous. You never know when you might get run over by a bus."

Irritation steamrolled over her earlier fear. "Why do I have the feeling that more people are killed by guns every year than run over by buses?" She folded her arms across her chest and gave him a long challenging look.

Dash shrugged. "Perhaps," he acknowledged reluctantly. "But that's because most people don't know how to handle them properly."

"And you do." It was not a question. From the moment she'd seen it in his hand, Claren had known that this was a man accustomed to the violence that came with such a deadly-looking weapon.

"Yes. I do."

Only three short words. But they spoke volumes. A long, drawn-out silence settled over them. Claren was the first to break it.

"I'm going downstairs to make some coffee," she said with an aplomb she was a long, long way from feeling. "I'm always a zombie until I get my morning jolt of caffeine."

"I don't know," Dash drawled, relieved when she seemed willing to drop the subject of the damn gun. "I think you look great. Kind of cute and tousled."

Was he actually arrogant enough to think that one not very original compliment would make her forget that only minutes ago she'd had the horrid steel barrel of a gun pointed her way?

She pulled the sash on her robe tighter. "It's not going to work, MacKenzie."

"What's not going to work?"

"Trying to throw me off the track by telling me I look cute. And tousled." She practically bit the words off. "Why don't you take your shower," she suggested. "By then the coffee should be ready, and over breakfast you can tell me why you feel the need to sleep with a gun."

Turning her back on him, she went down the hall, the silk of the robe swishing seductively, outlining the firm lines of her legs.

Dash stood under the pelting hot water, trying out stories and rejecting them. This wasn't some airhead bimbo; Claren O'Neill Wainwright was an intelligent, perceptive woman. Rubbing himself dry with a fragrant blue bath towel, he knew that she'd see through an out-and-out lie.

But as Dash yanked on his jeans, he also acknowledged that he couldn't tell her the truth. Not without undermining months of undercover work and possibly endangering lives.

The thing to do, Dash had decided by the time he reached the kitchen, was to tell Claren enough to allay her suspicions without blowing the entire operation—an operation that included agents from four continents and ten different governments—sky-high.

He was relieved when there was no outward sign of her earlier anger. She greeted him with a smile and placed a mug of hot, steaming coffee, a bowl of fresh berries and a perfectly toasted English muffin in front of him.

"This looks great," he said enthusiastically.

"I'm so glad you approve," she said with saccharine sweetness, "since I spent at least three minutes slaving over a hot toaster oven."

He took a drink of coffee and was surprised to find it as strong and black as he liked it. Too many women brewed coffee with the wimpy strength of herbal tea. "It's the thought that counts."

"Speaking of thoughts," she said, eyeing him over the rim of her own mug, "I believe it's time I told you about Elliott."

That, Dash considered, was an excellent idea. If she spent the morning ragging on her former fiancé, perhaps she'd forget about the gun. "You don't have to if you don't want to."

She smiled. "Oh, but I do. Because, as you'll soon see, there's a moral to my little tale of woe. One I believe you should understand before this goes any further."

"Before what goes any further?"

"Our relationship."

Dash had always considered *relationship* to be one of those talk-show female words. Lord knows, his wife had constantly harped about all the things that were wrong with theirs. "I didn't realize we had a relationship."

Liar, Claren thought. "I met Elliott when I first arrived in Seattle. In a way, he was my lifeline. I also considered him a paragon of virtue. So much so that I spent twelve years trying to fit myself into his extreme narrow mold."

"Must have been tough," Dash mumbled around a mouth of muffin.

"It was. But I thought I was in love." Claren had been thinking about it all night. "I now realize that it was simply a crush that I never outgrew."

"And that's why you called off the wedding?"

"No."

"So what happened? Did you catch him in the arms of a stripper the night before the big day?"

Dash couldn't remember his own bachelor party. But the following day his best man—Julia's brother—had assured him that he'd enjoyed himself immensely.

"Close." Claren felt her temper beginning to flare all over again. She took a drink of coffee, popped a plump juicy blackberry into her mouth and struggled for calm. "Although I don't want to sound immodest, our wedding was the social event of the season. Needless to say, several society reporters were in attendance."

Dash remembered that. All too well. "That figures."

"Yes." Her smile was tight and failed to reach her eyes. "Well, one reporter in particular, an annoying young man from the *Seattle Observer*—a tacky little tabloid shopper specializing in sensationalism—asked me what I thought of the lawsuit filed that morning against my husband-to-be."

"Someone was suing Byrd?" Dash asked, irritated that St. John's army of investigators hadn't uncovered a potential lawsuit. "For what?"

Emerald sparks flared in her eyes. "Actually it was a paternity suit."

It was all Dash could do not to spit his coffee across the table. "You're joking."

"I didn't find it a joking matter. Neither did Elliott, naturally."

"Naturally," Dash agreed. "I take it he denied it."

"Oh, yes. He was adamant that the child couldn't possibly be his."

"He wouldn't be the first guy to deny fooling around," Dash pointed out.

"That's where you're wrong," she countered. "Elliott didn't deny sleeping with the woman. He did, however, deny fathering her child."

"And you didn't believe him. So you called the wedding off."

"But I did believe him. Because he had absolute proof that although he had gone to bed with the woman, on numerous occasions, it turns out, he couldn't possibly be the child's father."

"A blood test?"

"Something more conclusive than that. The fact of the matter was that Elliott had had a vasectomy."

There was more to this. Something he still couldn't get a handle on. "That would do it," Dash agreed. "I take it he hadn't let the woman in on his little snip job."

"Actually," Claren said, her voice turning tight and coldly furious, "he hadn't let any of the women in his life know about his surgery."

Dash lifted a black brow. "Are you saying—"

"Elliott knew I wanted children—I talked about it all the time—and he purposely chose to deceive me. That's why I didn't go through with the marriage," she said. "And that is also when I realized that the man I'd thought I'd fallen in love with was nothing but a self-indulgent, egocentric fake. A fake and a liar.

"So now you know why I spent my wedding night alone," she said, looking Dash straight in the eye. "And you also know that the one thing I cannot—will not—put up with is someone lying to me. So," she said, giving him a smile he didn't quite trust, "why don't you tell me exactly why you're carrying that horrid-looking gun around?"

"It's a long story."

She put her elbows on the table, linked her fingers together and rested her chin on her joined hands. "I'm not going anywhere."

Realizing that he'd pushed himself into a very tight corner, Dash proceeded to try to extricate himself. "Did Darcy tell you what ship he was looking for?"

"The *Maria Theresa*," she said promptly. "She was a Spanish galleon that reportedly foundered in a hurricane in 1724. Other reports have her looted, then sunk by pirates. Known by treasure seekers as a 'ghost galleon,' she's been rumored to lie in several different places, from off Puerto Rico in the Atlantic, to Cuba, Vera Cruz and the Dominican Republic in the Caribbean. One report has her sunk off the northeast coast of South America."

So Darcy did share his passion with his niece in detail. Dash found that idea both interesting and unsettling. The more he got to know her, the more Dash wanted to believe that St. John was wrong about this woman's being involved in such a heinous crime.

"Do you know what she was supposedly carrying?"

"Quicksilver, which was needed by the Spanish to amalgamate gold and silver from New World ore,"

Claren answered. "Along with wine, gunpowder, personal effects of crew and passengers—many of whom were wealthy Cuban plantation owners—and several exquisite gifts from the governor of Nueva Isabela, which is now Santo Domingo, to Louis, the new king of Spain. Even if the ship had arrived back in Lisbon safely, Louis would have been dead, and his father, Philip V, would have returned to the throne, but I suppose it all would have just stayed in the family. Especially since there were also gifts meant for other members of the Bourbon family.

"The *Maria Theresa*, by the way, was named for King Philip's grandmother. Philip inherited the throne through her brother Charles II. And what does all this have to do with that gun?"

She was going after him like a bull terrier with a bone. "You've got your history down pat," he said. "But what do you know about the legend surrounding the ship?"

"About there also having been slaves smuggled aboard the *Maria Theresa*? And that their spirits haunt the ship, even now, bringing slow, painful deaths to anyone who tries to board?" she asked. "I don't believe it. And you're still not answering my question." Her eyes widened in disbelief. "Surely you don't believe ghosts killed Darcy?"

"No," Dash agreed. "I don't. But I do think there's a possibility that he was killed by men who wanted to claim the *Maria Theresa* for their own. And that they used a convenient legend to cover their tracks."

"That's ridiculous."

"I don't think so," Dash said quietly. Firmly. "I also think that there's a very good chance those same men might want to get rid of anyone else who knows too much about Darcy's expedition."

Color drained from her cheeks as his words slowly sank in. "Are you talking about me? You actually believe that someone might try to kill me?"

"Yes." Both his voice and his expression had turned deadly serious. "I do."

6

"WHO ARE YOU?" Claren's voice was thin, thready. "And more to the point, what are you?"

"I told you, I'm Dash MacKenzie. Darcy's friend."

"He never mentioned you."

"He had me witness his will," Dash pointed out.

"A handwritten will written on a water-stained yellow legal sheet. How do I know you didn't force him to write it? At gunpoint."

"Because if I'd forced him to write it," Dash retorted, "wouldn't I have been more likely to make myself the beneficiary? Instead of you?"

He had a point. But Claren couldn't quite overcome the feeling that he hadn't been completely honest with her from the beginning. "You could always force me to make out a will leaving my inheritance to you," she said slowly. "And then, if something happened to me, you'd end up with everything. Or," she said as the unsavory idea suddenly occurred to her, "you could marry me. Then you wouldn't even have to bother with the will, since a husband is automatically a beneficiary."

"Dammit!" Dash slammed his hand down onto the table. He stood up abruptly, causing his chair to overturn. "You've definitely been watching too many made-for-television movies. Do you actually believe I'd be capable of killing you?"

Actually she didn't. But from the deft way he'd handled that gun, she had the uneasy feeling that he'd used it before.

"While you're busy trying to solve a crime that hasn't even happened, Ms. Perry Mason," he ground out, "you'd better factor in the fact that I haven't mentioned marriage once."

Watching the muscle jerk in his cheek, Claren was sorry she'd brought up the subject. "I'm sorry," she said. "It's just that I'm not accustomed to having a gun pointed at me. It's also a little unsettling to hear that you think Darcy was murdered when I'm still trying to come to grips with the idea of him drowning. And I'm definitely not accustomed to hearing that my life might be in danger."

Struggling for calm and trying to make sense of all this, she leaned back in her chair and took a long, soothing sip of her cooling coffee. "Is that really why you came? To protect me?"

Dash was finding it harder and harder to look into those soft green eyes and lie. He was definitely getting soft; if he wasn't careful, he'd end up getting them both killed.

"That's part of the reason," he answered truthfully. "I knew if I let anything happen to you, Darcy would haunt me for the rest of my life."

"And the other reason?"

"I told you," he hedged, "I've always wanted to see the Northwest."

There was something he wasn't telling her. Claren could sense that he was holding back. But she was still too shaken by his revelation to dwell on it. "How long will you be staying?"

"As long as it takes," he answered enigmatically.

She sighed, tired of trying to understand anything about Dash MacKenzie. "What would you have done if I'd gotten married yesterday?"

"It wouldn't have changed a thing. I was all set to go to Hawaii. In fact, I'd booked a seat right behind you. On the aisle."

"You were going to—what do they call it?—keep me under surveillance during my honeymoon?"

"I was going to do whatever it took to keep you safe."

There was a quiet strength in his statement that fascinated Claren. "You really mean that," she said in quiet wonder.

"It's a man's responsibility to protect the weaker sex."

Claren lifted a tawny brow. "The weaker sex being women?"

"Of course."

"You'll excuse me if I don't subscribe to that theory?"

He'd suspected that she wouldn't. "You can argue the point all you like, Irish, but that doesn't change a thing. Oh, I know that you're pretty damn strong for a woman," he allowed. "But there are still some things that you need to be protected from."

God help her, even as she knew she should be screaming bloody murder at his outdated macho beliefs, Claren found herself actually enjoying this argument. "Such as?"

"How about murder, for a start?"

They were back to that again. Claren combed her fingers distractedly through her hair. "That's some start," she murmured.

For some reason, although he continued to insist that she was in danger, Claren didn't feel afraid. Then she looked up into his granite face, looked deep into his wolf-gray eyes and knew why. "That's what you were talking about last night, isn't it?" she asked softly. "About it being your duty to protect me."

"I realize that a modern career woman like yourself might find that idea ridiculous, but—"

"You're wrong." Claren stood up and put her hand on his arm. "I don't find it ridiculous at all. Actually I find it rather sweet."

"Sweet?" he roared. "You think I'm sweet?"

From his outburst, Claren realized that she'd struck a very sensitive nerve. "Wrong word, huh?"

"Horrendously wrong word," Dash agreed. "But you did manage to get your point across. You're not taking this at all seriously, are you?"

"I think you're serious," Claren allowed.

"But you also think I'm crazy."

"Not crazy. Just mistaken."

He shook his head, wondering why he'd thought things would be at all easier once he got them out in the open. "For both our sakes, Irish," he said, "I hope you're right."

But Dash didn't think so. Not even a little bit.

THEY SPENT the remainder of the day shopping. Dash followed Claren from store to store, watching her exchange greetings and accept condolences with the proprietors. That she was loved in the small, insular town was obvious. That Darcy had also been loved was equally clear.

They had lunch at a small café next to the ferry dock. The food was Chinese, and there was a lot of it. "Do you always eat like this?" Dash asked after he'd watched

Claren single-handedly devour a bowl of hot-and-sour soup, an entire order of pot stickers, shrimp fried rice and Kung Pao chicken.

"I told you," Claren said, "shopping always makes me hungry. Aren't you going to eat your egg roll?"

"It's all yours." Dash pushed the plate across the table.

"Thanks. Actually, to tell the truth, I don't usually eat so much," she admitted. "I don't know why, but ever since yesterday I've been absolutely starving."

She was wearing a brightly hued, off-the-shoulder dress that reminded Dash of gypsies. Seeing her like this, he found it impossible to imagine her in the dark tailored suits that she claimed had made up her wardrobe.

"Perhaps it's repressed passions."

"Perhaps," she said mildly. Deciding it was time to change the subject, she asked, "Now that I know the reason for you being here, I don't suppose you want to work around the house."

"Hey," Dash said, "we had a deal. You needed a handyman and I needed work."

"You only accepted my job offer so you could stay at the house and keep an eye on me. For Darcy."

"It may have started out being about Darcy, but things have changed." Dash handed her his fortune cookie. "Whether you want to believe it or not, I have my own reasons for not wanting anything to happen to you."

Claren couldn't believe his preposterous story about her life being in danger. That unpalatable thought kept her from dwelling on exactly how Dash's feelings toward her might have changed since yesterday.

"I still think—"

"It's not your job to think," he said, cutting her off with a sharp gesture. "It's your job to obey your uncle's dying wish and paint pretty pictures."

"And you'll do all the thinking."

"You got it." He folded his arms over his chest and gave her a long hard look that Claren was sure must make other women quake in their pumps.

She could feel her temper begin to fray again, strand by delicate strand. What was it about this man that had her constantly swinging from desire to fury? That's what she got, she decided, inviting a wolf into her house, into her life. "How on earth did I ever survive without you?" She cracked open the cookie with more force than necessary, scattering crumbs over the white tablecloth.

"Beats me." Dash plucked the slim white paper from between her fingers. "He is mad who trusts in the tameness of a wolf," he read aloud.

No. It had to be a joke. The man couldn't possibly read her mind. Claren drew in a quick, sharp breath and snatched the fortune from his fingers. "It really says that," she said, staring in disbelief at the words printed on the paper.

Dash had watched the color drain from her cheeks and wondered at the cause. "I'll admit it's a little unusual," he agreed. "A fortune cookie quoting Shakespeare, but—"

"This is Shakespeare?"

"From *King Lear*. It goes on to say that a man is also mad who believes in a horse's health, a boy's love or a whore's oath."

Claren didn't know which surprised her most. The fact that the fortune coincidentally mentioned a wolf at the very same time she was mentally comparing him to the animal, or that this man, professing to be no more than an itinerant handyman—a handyman with a gun—could quote Shakespeare. First Oscar Wilde, then the bard. Amazing.

"I can't figure you out," she said, shaking her head.

Dash refilled the blue-and-white teacup. "Just because I took an intro to Shakespeare class my plebe year—"

"Your what?"

Damn. What was it about this woman that had him forgetting everything he'd learned? "I took a class on Shakespeare's tragedies my freshman year in college. What's so surprising about that?"

"You didn't say freshman year," Claren said. "You said 'plebe year.' You went to the naval academy."

He felt the steel door of the trap closing shut and fought against it. "Yeah, I did."

"Why didn't you tell me?"

"Because you didn't ask."

"That's not an answer."

"Okay." St. John was going to kill him for this. "I didn't tell you because you didn't ask for past employment history."

"Are you in the navy now?"

"No."

"Are you CIA?"

"CIA? Come on, Irish, give me a break. Where do you get these wild ideas, anyway?"

"You're a fine one to be talking about wild ideas, Dashiell MacKenzie," she retorted, "after telling me that dear Darcy died because of the curse of the *Maria Theresa*."

"I didn't say the curse killed him."

"Oh, that's right. The truth of the matter is that the killers wanted us to think the ghosts murdered Darcy. And now they're coming after me." She tossed her hair over her shoulders. "You didn't answer my question. Are you CIA? Is that why you're so interested about what happened to Darcy? Because he stumbled into something dangerous on the island?"

She was getting too damn warm for comfort. "I'm not CIA," he insisted tightly. "Nor am I FBI, DEA, IRS or any other governmental initials you might think up."

"Then who do you work for?"

"At the moment I'm working for you. And if we don't get going right now, I'm not going to have time to go by the hardware store before it closes."

He pulled out his wallet and tossed some crisp new bills on the plastic tray. "In case you haven't noticed, Irish, one of the front steps is loose. I thought I'd fix it before you break that lovely, albeit stubborn, neck."

Frustrated by the way he insisted on total control, Claren had no choice but to follow him out of the restaurant.

She sulked as she trailed after him, watching with silent admiration as the order he gave to the hardware clerk displayed a surprising amount of knowledge of household repairs. Before they got out of the store, two different customers had come up to him asking for instructions on how to repair a leaking roof and a stopped-up garbage disposal. Perhaps he really was a handyman, after all, Claren considered. Of course he was. And she was Princess Di.

By the time the stores had closed, Claren had finished her own shopping and had filled the trunk and the back seat of Dash's rental car with bags filled with a variety of paints—oils, watercolors, acrylics and pastels. She'd also bought thinner, a variety of different-sized canvases, an easel, chalk, several sketch pads and enough brushes to make Dash consider that a great many sable had had to die to provide the world with art.

"You certainly bought enough paint," he said on the drive back to Darcy's house.

"I don't know where my talent lies," she said. Still irritated at him, she directed her gaze out the passenger window, pretending an interest in the curtain of dark green Douglas fir lining the roadway. "So I thought I should be prepared for anything."

"Makes sense to me. May I ask a question?"

"What?"

"Are you going to give me the silent treatment all night?"

"I'm not giving you the silent treatment."

"The hell you aren't. Are you mad at me just because I know a few Shakespeare quotes? Don't you think that's overreacting a bit?"

"I'm not angry about the Shakespeare. All right," she admitted reluctantly, "perhaps I am, just a little. But I'm more envious than angry. My major was business administration and hotel management. I only took the liberal-arts classes that were required, and sometimes, when I'm around people who can throw quotes around like confetti, I get a little self-conscious."

Her aunt and uncle, along with dear old Elliott, had really done a number on her self-confidence. Dash angrily wondered if she truly didn't know what a remarkable woman she was.

"I took a few classes," he said offhandedly. "Fortunately I have one of those memories that never gives anything up. It's more a parlor trick than literary criticism. And as for your lack of education, how many people do you think can run a hotel?" Before she answered, he said, "I've been meaning to ask you about that. How did you choose hotel management in the first place?"

"My parents ran a little inn in County Clare. It helped pay for the horse farm. It was nothing like a Whitfield Palace," she said, warming to the subject. "It was more personal, like a bed and breakfast, but my mother served three meals a day. We lived in the inn, and I loved helping her. She always believed that a guest should be as comfortable as he was in his own home, only more so."

"Sounds like a nice place to stay."

"It was," she said. "And it was a wonderful place to live. My mother had a way of making people feel welcome, like part of the family. I've tried to do that at the hotel, but, of course, it's harder when you're talking about three thousand guests instead of five or six."

The tension between them had dissipated. Instead, there was a comfortable feeling of companionship that almost made Dash forget what he was doing here in the first place. At this moment, alone with her in the car as the sky around them gradually darkened, he could almost believe that his sole purpose in coming to Seattle was to meet her.

"Do you believe in fate?" she asked. "Or destiny?"

He glanced over at her, surprised. "Darcy didn't tell me that one of your talents was mind reading. I was just thinking about fate."

"And? Do you believe in it?"

"I didn't," Dash said frankly as he pulled up the curving driveway and parked the car in front of the house. "But lately I'm beginning to wonder."

SOMEONE HAD BEEN BUSY while they were in town. The house looked as though a hurricane had blown through it. Furniture had been overturned, desk drawers emptied, Oriental vases smashed. Paper and broken glass littered the floor like confetti.

"Why?" she whispered.

Dash's first thought was to get Claren out of here now, in case the intruders were still inside. But that was unlikely. Since the road was a private one, ending here at the house, the vandals would have had to pass Dash and Claren on the way back to the highway. His hand, which had instinctively reached for the pistol at the small of his back, under his leather bomber jacket, returned to his side.

"I can't believe this." Stunned, Claren roamed through the house, from room to room, staring at the destruction. When she got to the paneled library, she gasped in dismay.

The furniture had been slashed; the white stuffing strewn over the oak floor resembled fallen snow. Paintings had been ripped from their frames, the canvases torn. Claren reached down and picked up one small canvas depicting the towering rock stacks along the windswept Washington coast.

"I remember when Darcy painted this," she murmured, running her fingers over the storm-tossed sea. "It was my birthday, and Aunt Winifred had planned a sweet-sixteen party at the country club. But then Darcy showed up, nearly kidnapped me—which didn't take much convincing—and took me clamming." Her sad smile was softly reminiscent.

It sounded like Darcy, Dash decided. Hell-bent for breaking society's rules. Including one as sacrosanct in certain circles as a sweet-sixteen party. "Aunt Winnie must have loved that."

"I was grounded for a week." Claren carefully put the painting down on the top of the nearby pigeonhole desk. All the drawers were missing. Looking around, she located two of them in the fireplace. "It was worth it."

A sob escaped her lips when she viewed the books that had been pulled from the library shelves. Dropping to her knees on the rag rug, she picked up one particular text and ran her fingers over the embossed leather cover. The binding had been broken; pages had been torn and scattered everywhere.

"Uncle Darcy loved these books," she said on something close to a whisper. "He spent his entire life collecting them." Sighing, she picked up another and began leafing through the remaining pages. "A lot of them are first editions."

Dash felt he understood Darcy's obvious passion for collecting. His wife had shared the same obsession; dealers in London, Milan, Rome and New York always lit up like Christmas trees whenever she walked into their shops. Afterward, however, once she had the object in question back home, her interest seemed to dwindle. Dash had realized early in their marriage that what excited Julia was the buying, not the having.

Growing up as the daughter of one of New York's earliest settlers, Julia Van Pelt had enough money to buy whatever she wanted. And for a time she'd wanted Dash. Unfortunately, although he hated to admit it even to himself, Dash knew that he'd made it easy for her. Because at the time he'd definitely been for sale.

"First editions are too valuable to leave hanging around a house that's vacant most of the year. He should have kept them in a safe-deposit box."

"Darcy didn't collect the books for their financial value," she said stiffly, needing to defend her uncle, who wasn't here to stand up for himself. "He searched for first editions the same way he searched for lost treasure."

She picked up a leather-bound copy of *Huckleberry Finn* and remembered the first time he'd read the story to her and how she'd wanted to run away just like Huck. "He believed that since first editions were printed right after they were written, they still carried the energy of the author."

She caught sight of Dickens's *The Old Curiosity Shop,* the pages ripped from their bindings. "And he didn't keep them locked away, because he wanted to be able to read them whenever he felt like it." By chance she picked up the very page where Little Nell died just as Kit Nubbles arrived to save her.

Dash saw her eyes well with tears. "You look pale." For the first time, he could view a light sprinkling of freckles across the bridge of her nose, along the slant of her cheekbones. "I'd better get you some water before you faint."

Claren looked up at Dash, as if she was surprised to see him standing there. Immersed in her distress, she'd almost forgotten his presence. "I told you I never faint."

She'd straightened her back, but Dash could still see the lingering shadow of shock in her wide green eyes, and her milkmaid complexion was the color of old parchment. He could accept and appreciate her obstinacy; after all, he had always possessed that personality trait himself.

He could handle her temper; in fact, he found her occasional displays of anger exciting. But as he looked down at her sitting there, looking so very vulnerable, so defenseless, he felt a deep pull of unfamiliar tenderness.

"And I told you that there's always a first time," he said gruffly, fighting the unwelcome emotion. "Wait here. I'll be right back."

He wasn't surprised to find the kitchen in the same condition. The pantry had been torn apart; the food had been taken out of the refrigerator, dumped into the sink and left to rot. Dishes, glasses and cutlery had been swept from open shelves.

Broken pieces of earthenware crunched like ice-crusted snow beneath his feet as Dash made his way to the sink. A plastic cup lay abandoned on the expansive white ceramic counter; after running the discarded food down the garbage disposal, he rinsed out the glass and filled it with cold water.

Before returning to the library, he picked up the ivory wall phone, surprised to find it working. Someone, he considered, had been careless. With a long, weary sigh, he dialed the familiar number.

"We've got a problem," he said when the phone was answered on the first ring. "Yeah, she's with me. But someone was at the house today.... The place looks like London after the blitz. From the appearance of the stuff they left in the sink, we're only a few hours behind them, so I'm taking her to a hotel in case they come back."

Dash listened to the heated protest he'd known was coming. "Look, St. John," he ground out, "she's innocent...I just know it," he insisted when the voice on the other end of the line demanded proof. "There was a time when you trusted my intuition," he reminded the man who'd once been his mentor and his superior. But that had been a long time ago, and Dash wasn't accustomed to taking orders any more now than he had been then.

"Look, I'm not going to use her as a sitting duck." His voice rose to a shout. Worried that Claren might hear him, he quickly lowered it again. "I can crack this case some other way, so just get off my back and let me get back to work."

That said, he hung up without waiting for an answer.

She was just where he'd left her, sitting on the rag rug in the middle of the room, bits and pieces of what was left of Darcy's beloved book collection on her lap. Seeing her like that, looking so small and lost, Dash experienced a surge of emotion stronger than the suspicion, the irritation or even the desire that Claren had instilled in him from the beginning.

As he crossed the room to her, Dash considered how ironic it was that this woman's vulnerability could ultimately bring about his downfall.

"Here." He shoved the glass into her hands and curled her fingers around it. "Drink up. It'll make you feel better."

He needed a drink himself. Something a lot stiffer than water. As if reading his mind again, Claren said, "There's a trick cupboard in the middle of the bookcase. Darcy used it as a bar."

"Trust Darcy not to keep anything simple." As he ran his hands over the wood, searching for the control, Dash both marveled at Darcy's ingenuity and wondered what other little tricks the old man had had up his sleeve. The back of the bookcase suddenly gave way, revealing a liquor cabinet. While well stocked, it was definitely limited in selection.

"Didn't Darcy drink anything but Irish whiskey?" In Jamaica the elderly man had enjoyed his Irish, but had also displayed a liking for Mai Tais and rum punches. "Wait a minute," he said before Claren could answer. "I may have found something."

The bottle was still in its Christmas wrapping. "The card was signed by someone named Maxine," Dash said.

"Maxine runs the dress shop. She's been trying to seduce Darcy for ages. Ever since her husband died."

Dash thought about the barmaid who'd tumbled ever so willingly into bed with Darcy back in Jamaica. For a man pushing seventy, Darcy O'Neill certainly hadn't been one to let age slow him down.

"Candy's dandy," Dash murmured, pouring the brandy into one of the balloon glasses.

"But liquor's quicker," Claren finished up. "You should do that more often."

"Do what? Would you like a drink?"

She answered his second question first. "I think I would. Smile," she said, responding to his first question. "You have a very attractive smile," she told him with her newfound frankness. "It's incredibly sexy. If you used it more often, you'd undoubtedly have women throwing themselves at your feet. Not that you probably don't already," she mused, thinking of the way the waitress last night had practically worn a neon Available sign around her neck. "But even so, it's quite effective."

"Thank you. I guess." Dash was amused in spite of himself. In spite of their situation. He splashed some of Darcy's brandy into a second snifter. "Do you always talk off the top of your head?"

"No. Actually I'm usually quite circumspect." She waited for him to laugh.

He didn't. "I have trouble believing that." The color was returning to her cheeks. Deciding to get her out of here as soon as he finished his drink, Dash sat down beside Claren on the rug.

"It's true," she insisted. "I'm also incredibly boring."

"Now, that is impossible to believe." Knowing that he was treading on quicksand, but unable to resist, he ran his knuckles in a slow, warm sweep up her cheek. "You are many things, Irish. But boring is definitely not one of them."

Dash read the sensual appeal in the swirling dark green depths of her eyes. There was desire there. And temptation. But most of all, he saw danger.

She took a sip of brandy and tried to tell herself that it was the liquor creating the slow warmth spreading through her body. Lifting her hand, Claren ran her own fingers over the strong bones of his face, over the taut skin darkened to the hue of mahogany by the bright Caribbean sun. The ebony shadow of a day's growth of beard felt like the finest-grade sandpaper against her fingertips.

"I've been wondering about something."

Dash's eyes brushed over her mouth, lingering there for a long, suspended moment before returning to her eyes. Against his will, he was fascinated by the wealth of emotions that came and went in those remarkable green eyes.

"What?" His voice was harsh and rough.

"What it would be like to have you kiss me." There. She'd said it.

"I already know."

Even as he told himself he should back away now while he still could, Dash found himself drawn to the pale pink softness of her mouth. A mouth that soft, that full, was designed to tempt a man. Throwing back his head, he tossed off the brandy and put the empty glass down on the floor beside him.

He took hold of her shoulders, whether to pull her close or push her away he could not decide. "Kissing you, Irish, would be pure trouble."

Claren looked into his gray eyes and saw a storm brewing. His irises darkened until they were nearly as dark as the pupils. Her lips parted. She put her own glass down beside his, then drew in a deep breath and held it, waiting.

They only had to move. A slight shifting of their heads, and their lips would meet. Dash told himself all the reasons why this would be a mistake.

And then he covered her mouth with his.

The intensity rocked them both. This was no gentle first kiss. There was no slow, smoldering warmth. The passion ignited instantly, causing a hot, urgent flow of desire. Dash's mouth craved passion; in response, sweet passion flowed from Claren into him. His hands, running up and down her arms, sought submission; she melted quickly into the heated kiss, her body following her reckless heart, offering herself unconditionally.

His mind demanded strength; her hands were in his hair, clenching, refusing to let him take without giving. Of all the women Dash had ever known, he'd never been with one who matched him so perfectly. Hunger answered hunger; need answered need.

The more he took, the more he gave, the more Dash craved. His teeth nipped, his tongue plunged, his hands aroused. He'd never known a woman who let her emotions flow so freely; they crested higher and higher until he was drowning in them.

Dash was no stranger to danger, to risk. He'd lived with it, and for a time had even enjoyed it. But this woman, and the feelings she stirred in him, represented more risk than he'd ever known. He'd always recognized his own strengths, his own weaknesses.

But now, even as he fought to remember that he damn well didn't want Claren O'Neill Wainwright in his life, Dash was forced to admit that she represented a major weakness. At the very time he could least afford one.

Her lips were even softer than he'd imagined. And smooth. A low moan flowed from between those lips into him; Dash was rocked more by that soft sound than by any other sexual encounter he'd experienced.

As his mouth ravaged her, as his hands stoked hidden fires burning deep within her, Claren knew that nothing would ever be the same again. Needs welled up inside her, years of emptiness waiting to be filled. She hungered, starved, for more.

He hadn't meant to touch her. And he damn well hadn't meant to kiss her. But now that he had, Dash promised himself that the memory of the heated kiss would have to last a lifetime. Because it had been a mistake. One he didn't intend to make again.

Dash drew back, denying the clamoring demands of his mutinous body. His breath was fast and shallow, and he felt as if he'd just come to a screeching stop at the edge of a towering granite cliff. "We'd better get going."

Breathless herself, and aching, Claren stared at him. "Go? Where?" Her head was spinning; coherent thought had deserted her. "Why?"

Her cheeks were flushed, her lips dark, her eyes clouded with desire. Looking at her this way, Dash imagined he could see the jagged, deadly rocks of the steep drop below.

"I'm taking you back to town." The hell with orders—he wouldn't relax until she was somewhere safe.

Her mind was gone, Claren realized. Dash had stolen it, along with her heart and her soul during that frightening, exhilarating kiss. "Why?"

"Look around you. The reason should be quite obvious."

She blinked, trying to force her whirling mind into focus. "I know it's a mess," she admitted. "But surely we can find a room upstairs that's not too bad."

"Dammit, I don't care that it's a mess." He stood up and glared down at her. Fear for her safety, and frustration at the situation he found himself in, made his own temper flare.

"You don't have to yell," Claren said. As she looked up at him, it crossed her mind once again that it was a good thing she enjoyed puzzles. Because Dash MacKenzie was by far the most baffling man she'd ever met.

"Don't you understand?" he ground out, his hands curled into fists at his side. "Whoever trashed this place could come back."

"They won't."

"Now she's an expert on the criminal mind," he muttered.

For the sake of peace, Claren opted to ignore his sarcastic statement. She stood up, as well, and put her hand on his arm, feeling the muscle tense beneath her light touch.

"They were vandals, Dash. If they'd been thieves, they would have stolen Darcy's things—they wouldn't have left everything strewn around. They've gotten their kicks, now they've moved on. We'll call the police, they'll come take a statement, and that'll be the end of it."

She was right about their not being thieves. At least, not in the conventional sense. Dash wondered what she'd say if he told her the truth and decided he couldn't risk it. Not until he got all the players in this deadly little melodrama straightened out.

"You may have a valid point. But I'm not taking any chances."

She folded her arms across her chest. "Fine. Then you go back to town alone."

Dash folded his own arms. "I'm not leaving here without you." The back-and-forth movement of his jaw suggested he was grinding his teeth.

"Well, I'm not going anywhere," Claren retorted.

That was it. Dash's thinly reigned patience tore. "That's what you think."

Scooping her up, he threw her over his shoulder, fireman's style, and began marching toward the front door.

"What do you think you're doing?" Furious, Claren beat her fists against his back, but for all the good it did her, she might as well have been hitting a brick wall.

"I'm taking you back to town."

"You'll never find a room," she warned. "I told you there's a jazz festival in town this weekend. People come from all over the country. Every place is booked weeks—months—in advance."

"There you go, underestimating me again," Dash said with a calm reassurance that Claren found infuriating. "Don't worry, Irish, you won't end up on the street. I'll find us a place to spend the night."

"You can't just drag me wherever you want," she insisted. "That's kidnapping."

"Probably is." He shifted her in his arms as he locked the front door behind them and reactivated the burglar alarm. He doubted if St. John's forensic guys would find anything, but he wanted to keep the place as clean as he could until they had a chance to go over it. "You can call all the cops you want and press all the charges you want when we get to Port Vancouver."

7

ONCE AGAIN she surprised him.

Since Port Vancouver served as the county seat, it was the home of the county sheriff's department. The office was located up the strait from the ferry wharf and across the street from the city hall and museum. From the size of the building, which also housed the jail, Dash decided that crime was not yet rampant in the area.

The sheriff, an attractive woman in her thirties, took the report of the break-in with unofficial-like sympathy. She also shared Claren's surprise; vandalism was an uncommon occurrence in a town where everyone knew his neighbor.

Dash wondered what else Claren was going to say. That she was furious was obvious; she'd fumed the entire drive to town, her anger surrounding her like a threatening thunderhead. He suspected that in a case of his word against hers, he'd land in one of the three jail cells. But not for long. Even if Claren did have him arrested for abduction, one phone call from St. John would spring him before she could blink those incredible green eyes.

But instead of pressing charges against him, Claren merely stated what little facts she knew about the break-in, answered the sheriff's questions as well as she could and returned to the car without uttering a single word about Dash's behavior.

"What happened to charging me with kidnapping?" he asked. "I thought you couldn't wait to have the cops toss me behind bars and throw away the key."

She turned to him, and Dash could see the lingering anger in her eyes. "You had no right dragging me out of my own house that way," she insisted. They were the first words she'd spoken to him since he'd carried her out to the car. "And I think you're overbearing and horribly chauvinistic. But this is between you and me. There was no reason to involve anyone else."

So she was a woman who fought her own battles. Somehow Dash had guessed that she would be. "You know, Irish," he said as he twisted the key in the ignition, "I like your style."

The casual words shouldn't have given her such pleasure. They shouldn't, Claren told herself over and over again. But heaven help her, they did.

She was right. Every place Dash tried was booked full.

"I hate to say I told you," Claren said when he came back to the car after being turned away by the Puffin & Gull Apartment Motel.

"You love it," Dash muttered.

"Perhaps we ought to go back to the house," she suggested sweetly.

"Not on a bet."

"But that was the last place to stay in town." She knew that either Maxine or Mildred or any of a number of townspeople would be happy to take her in. But although she was still furious at him for his autocratic behavior, Claren was curious to see what Dash was going to do next.

"No, it wasn't."

"But—" When he turned the car around and started in the opposite direction, headed back out of town, comprehension dawned.

It was a test, she decided as he pulled the car into the gravel parking lot. There was no way the man could be serious. The blinking sign advertised water beds, in-room adult movies and a vacancy. The *V* in Vacancy had burned out, but the sign still managed to get its point across. If the movies and the water beds weren't entertainment enough, an adult bookstore was located next door.

On the other side of the motel was a tavern. Built to resemble a log cabin, the bar had been appropriately named the Timberline. The marquee announced the appearance of a band whose name Dash did not recognize. Which wasn't surprising. After all, he'd been out of the country for a long time and, since this wasn't exactly a bustling hub of civilization, he suspected that the band would consist of local musicians.

"I can't believe it," Dash said as he cut the engine.

"Believe what?"

"That you're not screaming bloody murder."

She shrugged. In for a penny, in for a pound. Besides, she'd secretly longed to see the interior of the county's most infamous rendezvous location for years.

"I'm too exhausted to scream." That was definitely true. An old expression of her father's came to mind: rode hard and put away wet. That's exactly how she was feeling.

"You've had a bad shock, finding Darcy's house trashed like that," he said, not quite trusting her easy acquiescence. Thus far, nothing about this woman had been easy. "You could probably use some sleep." He pocketed the car key. "I'll go check in. Wait here."

She hated the way he had of issuing orders, as if he was accustomed to everyone snapping to attention for him. But, too tired to start another argument, Claren simply nodded her assent. Once he was gone, she leaned her head back against the seat and shut her eyes. Within seconds she'd fallen asleep.

"You're going to hit the roof." Dash's words jerked her from a light slumber.

"There was only one room," she guessed.

Having expected a furious tirade, Dash looked at her cautiously. She reminded him of the calm before the storm. "I know it's a cliché, but I swear, it's true."

Her eyelids had gone incredibly heavy. She could hardly hold them up. Even if there was another place to go, Claren was too tired to move. Merely getting to the door of the room would take all the strength she could muster. Privately she wondered if she could con Dash into carrying her into the room by refusing to budge.

Dash saw the faint smile flit across her lips and wondered at the cause.

Claren saw him looking at her and realized that he was waiting for an answer. "I believe you," she murmured sleepily.

She was exhausted. Her face, in the flashing red glow of the motel sign, looked unnaturally drawn and the light had gone from her eyes. She looked unbearably fragile. Something unbidden, unwanted, stirred inside him.

"Let's get you to bed."

Bed. It had to be the most marvelous word in the English language. Half-asleep already, Claren nodded her assent.

The room was beyond even Claren's wildest imagination. The walls were covered in red embossed velvet wallpaper; the carpeting was an unsettling blend of red and black and purple and dotted with innumerable cigarette burns. Gold-flecked mirrored squares on the ceiling reflected the enormous bed, which was covered in a fake velour tiger-skin bedspread.

The only other furniture in the room was a red velvet wing chair. Claren doubted that the usual occupants of this room missed having a chest of drawers.

"I didn't even know they made heart-shaped water beds," she murmured. Her attention was drawn to the wall over the immense bed, where a well-endowed nude blonde had been painted on black velvet.

"Live and learn." Dash went into the adjoining bathroom, satisfied yet not surprised to find that the narrow window had been barred. "It's not exactly the Kublai Khan's pleasure dome, but I suppose it'll have to do."

When he came out of the bathroom, Claren was standing beside the bed, right where he'd left her. He watched her fingers fumble clumsily with the buttons running down the front of her peasant dress. "Here, let me help."

Grateful for the assistance and trusting Dash perhaps more than she should, Claren obediently dropped her hands to her sides.

Although he knew he was playing with fire, Dash maneuvered each button through its hole while trying not to be moved by the growing expanse of ivory flesh he was exposing.

The dress slid to the carpeting in a puddle of multicolored gauze. Too exhausted to worry about modesty, Claren reminded herself wearily that the lace-trimmed teddy—another one of Maxine's brilliant suggestions—covered a great deal more than the bikini she'd worn water-skiing on Lake Washington last weekend.

The bodice of the scarlet silk teddy clung tenuously to her breasts. Dash knew that it would take only a casual motion of his hand to send it falling down around her waist. The urge to do exactly that, when her pallor revealed her absolute exhaustion, made him wonder what kind of man he'd become.

Perhaps, Dash considered, St. John had been right when he'd told him that he'd been away from civilization too long.

"I've got to go next door and get some cigarettes. I won't be long."

The reluctant note of caring in his voice made her smile. "Don't worry about me. I'll be asleep the minute my head hits the pillow."

Maybe one of them would sleep. But Dash knew that just the thought of her lying in that ridiculous bed, clad in that brief scrap of crimson silk, would be enough to keep him awake all night.

THE TIMBERLINE WAS like every other country-and-western bar in the country. A layer of cigarette smoke hung over the room like a shroud, the center of the floor was taken up by pool tables, two brightly colored pinball machines and a pay telephone stood against the far wall. Dusty bottles were lined up behind the bar, and beer signs glowed dimly in the smoky haze. On a small wooden platform at the back of the bar, a trio of musicians, dressed in snap-front Western shirts, faded jeans and cowboy boots, sang desolately of unfaithful women, hard days and even harder nights.

A lone woman, with wildly permed blond hair and wearing an off-the-shoulder black blouse and short black leather skirt, swayed dreamily to the music, apparently content to dance alone. Two men, loggers, Dash decided from their appearance, sat side by side on stools at the bar and watched the woman as they drank their beer from bottles, enjoying the free floor show. A lone elderly woman seated a few stools down from the loggers was engaged in conversation with the bartender.

Dash felt the blonde's gaze burning into his back as he made his way to the pay phone and knew that if he turned around he'd see an open invitation in her eyes. Dash was used to women wanting him; from the time a carhop down at the Burger Shack in Guthrie had seduced him on his fifteenth birthday, women had demonstrated an attraction to his size and what they always referred to as his dangerous looks. In his younger years Dash had taken advantage of their willingness to go to bed with him. These days he'd grown a great deal more choosy.

In fact, he considered thoughtfully as he punched the telephone buttons with more force than necessary, it had been more than six months since he'd had a woman. Perhaps all those months of celibacy were why he found himself so attracted to Claren. The idea made sense, Dash told himself. It also made him feel a hell of a lot better.

"We've moved to a motel," Dash said when St. John answered the phone. He listened to the complaint he'd known was coming. "Hey," he said when his superior's furious diatribe had finally run down, "this way you can get the forensics guys on the place without her suspecting a thing."

Dash glanced over at the poster that had been stapled to the wall next to the phone, and realized that the weekend jazz festival was the solution to his next problem. "Yeah, I can keep her away tomorrow," he assured St. John. "Just get the place cleaned up by nightfall, because I'm not certain I can keep her in this motel two nights running."

There was a time when he would have laughed at the sexual suggestion St. John proposed. There was also a time when he might have resorted to keeping Claren in bed if that's what it took to keep her under surveillance. But that was in another lifetime, a life he'd thought he'd put behind him. Until Darcy O'Neill had shown up in Jamaica and pulled him unwillingly back into the fray.

Cutting the conversation short, he hung up, ordered a beer and took a table by the window that offered a view of both the parking lot and the motel-room door.

Once again the thought of Claren alone in that enormous bed created a deep sexual pull. This time Dash comforted himself with the idea that it was not Claren who had him feeling this way. Any reasonably attractive woman would do.

"Didn't anyone ever tell you that it's not healthy to drink alone?"

He glanced up at the dancer, who was standing beside his table, her eyes bright, her smile inviting. She was, Dash realized with some surprise, actually quite attractive. Or she would be if she washed some of that makeup off her face. Her perfume, dark and musky and straightforward, was a decided contrast to Claren's light, tantalizing floral scent.

"I guess I'm just not in the mood for company tonight," he said. "Sorry."

She glanced out the window, following the direction of his earlier gaze. "You had a fight with your girl. I watched you check in," she explained at his quick, sharp look. "Sure didn't take you long to get kicked out."

"The woman has one hell of a temper," Dash said.

"She's also a damn fool to let you get away," the woman decided with a toss of her platinum head. She reached out and ran her fingers through his hair. "You could always try making her jealous."

Her voluptuous breasts, overflowing the bodice of her tight black blouse, were almost in his face, her perfume was surrounding him like a seductive cloud and her fingers were kneading the back of his neck with a warm, practiced touch. Dash waited with a certain fatalistic curiosity for his body to respond.

Nothing. *Nada.* Zip. So much for his theory about needing a woman. Any woman.

"Sorry, babe." He gave her an apologetic smile. "But I guess I'm just not in the mood tonight."

She licked her lips, giving him one last taste of what he was turning down. "You sure? Sometimes all it takes is the right woman."

She had hit just a little too close to home for comfort. "I'm sure." Frustrated with the way Claren had him feeling, Dash forgot his manners and turned back to watch the motel-room door.

"Well," the woman huffed, tossing her curly blond hair over her shoulder, "it's your loss, cowboy." Marching away on impossibly high-heeled black suede boots, she returned to her solitary dancing.

Dash wasn't aware of her leaving. Every ounce of his concentration, every atom of his body, was directed toward that ridiculously decorated room and the oversize heart-shaped bed.

After a second beer Dash decided that he'd waited long enough. Surely she'd be out like a light by now; after all, the woman had practically been asleep on her feet when he'd left.

Once again he was wrong. He heard the soft weeping the moment he entered the room. In the moonlight slanting through the window, he could see her, curled up in a tight little ball, her arms wrapped around the flat feather pillow, her shoulders shaking with her sobs.

"Claren." He turned on the lamp, bathing the room in an unearthly red glow, then sat on the edge of the water bed, starting off a series of violent waves. "It's going to be okay," he murmured, stroking her trembling pale shoulders. "Darcy's house will be cleaned up by this time tomorrow night."

"That's not what I'm crying about," she said into the pillow.

The room was warm, but she was unnaturally cold. Her skin was like ice. "Then, what?"

"It's Darcy." She surprised him by suddenly sitting up, flinging her arms around his neck and pressing her face against his shirt. "Oh, Dash," she sobbed, "he's not coming back. Darcy is really truly dead."

Dash wondered why realization had been so long in coming. After all, Darcy had been reported missing two weeks ago. But as she clung to him, sobbing harshly, he realized that, having not wanted to face the truth, she'd allowed the elaborate wedding preparations to numb her grief. Now finally the pain had broken through. Aided and abetted, he decided, by the unpalatable sight of the destruction of her uncle's beloved house.

Her tears were soaking the front of his shirt. Dash didn't say anything. Instead, he simply held her, waiting for her to cry out her grief. Grief that was long overdue.

When she ran out of tears, Claren remained silent for a long time, content to remain where she was, safe and secure in the circle of Dash's arms. She wondered how it was that Dash could be both strong and gentle at the same time. Elliott, she thought with a sad little sigh, had been neither.

"Thank you."

He ran his hand down her hair. "Hey," he said with forced composure, "I miss him, too."

She dashed at the moisture on her cheeks. "I don't know what I'm going to do without him," she admitted raggedly. "When you left for your cigarettes a little while ago, it suddenly dawned on me that I'm all alone."

He thought of reminding her about her aunt and uncle, then decided that wasn't what she was talking about. Families were not something genetic, like green eyes or red hair. Families consisted of people who truly cared about you, and about whom you cared, all of you watching out for one another, sharing the good times, as well as the bad, protecting each other from outsiders.

Dash hadn't had a big family, but he'd had his mother, who'd never whispered one word of regret at the way their life had turned out. She'd been a wonderful woman, soft and gentle and heartbreakingly frail. Dash had been with her at the end, holding her hand, begging her not to leave him. But she had.

That's when the orphaned five-year-old learned exactly how lonely the world could be. Considered a half breed because of his Cheyenne father, he'd been shunned by both races, forced to spend his youth in a variety of foster homes until the angry young boy finally landed, at age ten, in the Oklahoma Bible Fellowship home for wayward boys. Which was where he'd discovered exactly how cruel and brutal people could be.

He shook his head, irritated at the way Claren had him thinking of things he'd put behind him long ago.

"You have me," he heard himself saying.

Startled by the husky warmth in his voice, Claren tilted her head back and looked up at him with moist and shining eyes. "How long are you going to stay?"

Until I crack this case, he thought. Until I clear Darcy's name. Until I know that you're safe. "For as long as you need me," he said instead.

Hope was a hummingbird fluttering its delicate wings inside Claren's heart. And at that moment, as she basked in the warmth of his smoky gray eyes, she felt herself falling totally, inexorably in love.

Dash saw the hope and something else a great deal more dangerous in her gaze and cursed himself for having put it there. Now that the crisis had passed, he was starting to realize just how good—how right—she felt in his arms. He'd been right, her fragrant skin was softer than silk.

"You'd better get to sleep." He bent his head and kissed the top of her head. "We've got a big day ahead tomorrow."

"I know." Her bare shoulders sagged. "It's going to take forever to clean up that mess."

He moved his wide hand up and down her back, enjoying the feel of silk against his palm. "I was referring to the jazz festival that starts tomorrow morning."

It was the last thing she would have expected him to suggest. "The jazz festival?"

"You do like jazz, don't you?"

"Of course, but the house—"

"I've got all that taken care of. While we're enjoying the hot jazz and cool blues, a team of professionals is going to put Darcy's house back to the way it was. Probably a lot neater, considering your uncle's housekeeping skills."

"You hired a team of professionals?" Claren looked at him as if he were speaking a rare Martian dialect.

"I thought you hired me to take care of things around the house."

"I did, but—"

"So I was only doing my job. Come on, Claren, it'd take you and I at least a week to clean that place."

"True," she admitted, still dazed, "but when did you arrange this?"

"While I was out."

"Just now."

"Yep."

"But you don't know anyone around here," she persisted. There was something about this that was too easy. Too neat.

"Ever hear of the Yellow Pages?"

"But most businesses aren't open at—" she glanced down at the watch she'd forgotten to take off "—eleven o'clock at night."

He'd been so busy concentrating on her grief that Dash had almost forgotten exactly how frustrating this woman could be. "I took care of it," he ground out. "That's all you need to know."

Claren opened her mouth to protest his autocratic attitude, then shut it, deciding that to enter into an argument now would take more energy than she had.

Dash read her decision in her expressive face and was relieved. The way she'd had him swinging from caring to frustrated to sexually aching all day had taken its toll.

"Don't worry about it," he said, softening his tone. "Right now you need to get some rest."

Now that she could agree with. "Where are you going to sleep?"

He'd already considered that and had come to the conclusion that he wasn't about to test himself by sleeping in this ridiculous bed with Claren. "I'll just sack out in the chair."

She glanced over at the piece of furniture in question. "You're too big. You'll never be able to sleep."

She had a point. "Then I'll sleep on the floor."

Claren shuddered at that thought. "That carpet probably hasn't been cleaned since the Nixon administration." She shifted over and pulled back the shiny black polyester sheets in invitation. "It's a big bed, Dash. And I trust you."

Which showed how gullible the woman could be, Dash decided with a burst of self-revulsion. When St. John had come to him with the scheme, going back to work had been the last thing on Dash's mind. But after a great deal of argument, he'd reluctantly accepted the assignment, if for no other reason than to prove the innocence of the man who'd become his friend.

It had seemed so simple. Watch the niece and wait for something to happen. It hadn't bothered his conscience that he'd have to lie; Dash figured that whatever conscience he may have been born with had died along with his innocence a long time ago.

The job was not that different from so many others; the woman, Dash had told himself, would be no different from all the other women who'd passed through his life.

That's what he'd told himself. Unfortunately he'd been dead wrong. On both counts.

He carefully judged the distance from bed to door. Then he switched off the lamp, placed his pistol on the floor and finally, headed hell-bent into temptation, climbed between the slippery sheets. His weight started yet another tidal wave that sent Claren sliding into him.

Her flesh, so cold earlier, was as warm as summer sunshine. And as soft as the billowy white clouds found in those same summer skies. She seemed to melt into him; Dash could practically feel her bones liquify. She didn't immediately pull back; instead, from the way she looked up at him, her emerald eyes gleaming invitingly in the silvery moonlight, he knew that her surrender was imminent.

His hands curled around her shoulders. "Now I remember why I hate water beds." He shoved her over to her own side with a rough strength that belied his earlier gentleness. "Better get some sleep, Irish. You've had one hell of a couple of days."

Claren was hurt by his ungallant rejection, but after a short sulk she decided that it was all for the best. Because it was true that they were both tired. It was also true that he'd promised to stay. She was smiling as she drifted off.

THE SUN WAS SHINING through the slit in the red brocade draperies. Frustrated at the way the bright light had intruded on her sensual dream, Claren tried to turn her back to the window, only to find herself held captive by a heavy arm wrapped around her waist, a long leg crossed possessively over hers. It felt, she decided as she cuddled closer to Dash's solid bulk, wonderful.

He thought he was dreaming. But then he realized that the soft feminine body pressed so tightly against his was all too real. "I'm sorry," he muttered, pulling away.

"Don't be." Smiling, Claren ran her fingers over his face, enjoying the feel of his morning beard against her fingertips.

Dash jerked away and sat up against the padded velveteen headboard. His blistering scowl would have intimidated a lesser woman. "Dammit, Irish—"

Nothing had ever felt so right as the feeling she'd experienced waking up in Dash's arms. Having dreamed about the heated kiss they'd shared all night, Claren was ready for an encore. Sitting up, as well, she took confidence from the fact that he hadn't left the bed.

"I thought you wanted me," she said prettily as she traced the harshly cut line of his lips with a seashell-pink-tinted fingernail.

Desire flared, hot and restless. Even as Dash struggled to bank it down, he knew that to deny her soft statement was one lie even he couldn't pull off. "I do. I have from the beginning."

He grasped the tops of her arms. Hard. Whether to push her away or draw her closer, Dash could not decide. "But wanting and having are two different things. Dammit, Irish, this can't go anywhere."

Claren knew that her reckless behavior was totally against every tenet she'd been brought up to believe. But the way this man could make her feel, with a single touch, a lingering look, was like nothing she'd ever known. She knew that he was not a man to stay in one place for long. And knowing that, she felt that she had to take advantage of the emotions sparking between them now, before he moved on, taking with him erotic secrets she was desperate to know.

Dash knew those secrets. She'd seen it in his eyes, dark and dangerous and tempting. Tempting enough that she was willing—eager—to discard years of self-discipline, of rationality, to give herself to a man she'd just met.

"I'd say it already has."

"I'm not like Byrd," he warned.

"Thank goodness." Claren smiled. His fingers were digging into her flesh, but she refused to flinch. "If you were, we wouldn't be here," she murmured silkily. "Like this. You wanting me. Me wanting you."

Leaning forward, she brushed her lips against his. Offering sweet temptations.

Dash told himself he was a fool for turning down what she was so willingly offering. After all, hadn't he already determined to have her before this was over?

But that was before he'd come to realize that this was not the type of woman a man could easily walk away from. Dash was shaken by the intensity of his feelings, and he was wary of committing himself to something he didn't want to understand.

"Do you have any idea what the hell you're doing?"

"I'm trying to seduce you," she murmured as she scattered kisses from one corner of his frowning mouth to the other. "But you seem to be resisting." She tilted her head back to look up at him. "Am I doing something wrong?"

"Claren, there are a thousand—dammit—a million reasons why this is wrong."

"At least," she agreed, refusing to consider any of them. There would be time enough to face the consequences. "But I'm tired of being logical." Shifting, she caught his earlobe between her teeth. "I want to break all thousand, all million rules." Sighing, she pressed her body against him, soft female flesh to rigid male. "I want to break them with you, Dash."

Was that her heart pounding? Or his? Dash was on fire. He was trapped in a furnace without any way to escape. His fingers tightened on her arms; it took every ounce of his willpower to keep from shaking her. It took even more to keep from dragging her down to the mattress, stripping that little scrap of crimson silk from her and taking her with a ruthlessness that would leave them both breathless.

He decided to give her one last chance. "I won't treat you like a lady. I don't remember how. If I ever knew in the first place."

She found the lambent, strangely angry flame in his eyes exhilarating. Knowing that she was playing with fire and unable to resist, she laughed softly. "Is that supposed to frighten me away?"

Her eyes were emerald insolence. Passion too long denied blazed in her gaze. But along with the passion, he saw emotions too dangerous to categorize. She had no right to ask him for things he couldn't give. He had no right to want to give them to her.

Impatient, frustrated, aching, he dragged her closer. Passion overcame logic, and need trampled vigilance. She was right about one thing, Dash decided. The hell with the rules.

"Damn you, Irish," he groaned as his mouth savaged hers. With her scent, her smile, her soft eyes, she'd lured him deeper and deeper into quicksand until now he'd sunk in over his head. "Damn you and your crooked uncle."

8

THEY CAME together like thunder, lost in a storm of their own making. Dash knew it was insane to want—to need—Claren like this. He knew it would be madness to make love to her, knew it would complicate things beyond reason. But as her lips moved urgently over his face and her hands fretted against his hot, moist flesh, he decided that this was a woman worth going mad for.

She was on fire. Heat like nothing she'd ever known, or imagined, was building inside her. And outside. The air practically sparked with it. Claren had never known that a man and a woman could share something so dark, so incendiary. So dangerous. And even as the flames threatened to engulf her, she wanted more. Much, much more.

His hands ran bruisingly over her, heating the silk covering her to the melting point. The scent of passion rose to surround them, heady, arousing, erotic. All Claren's senses were heightened. She could taste the anger, the frustration, in his kiss. She felt his fingers struggling with the ribbon laces running down the front of the teddy; she heard him swear. When she heard the sound of silk tearing, she nearly wept with relief.

As a lover, he was everything she'd expected, dangerous, thrilling, terrifying. She'd thought she'd been prepared. She'd thought she'd known desire, understood passion. But at the first touch of his lips on her breast, Claren knew that she'd been wrong. She arched against his mouth and let her mind empty.

His fingers were cool, his mouth hot. The morning stubble of beard scraped against her skin like the finest grade of sandpaper, stimulating her flesh, arousing her desire. Incredibly, magically, he seemed to know just where she wanted him to touch, where she yearned to have his hands linger. When his lips followed those clever, wicked hands, Claren cried out in astonished delight. Her blood pumped hot and hard. Passion was a white-hot flame burning inside her.

Her name was torn from him on a moan of need. He ripped the torn teddy from her in a frenzy, his mouth devouring every bit of newly exposed skin. In the smoky haze surrounding her mind, Claren realized with an erotic start that his briefs were gone as well, whipped away, perhaps by the heated, rising winds. Hot flesh to hot flesh, mouth to mouth, they moved together, driving each other to the brink of sanity. And beyond.

He was lost in the grip of an impossible greed, an unbearable hunger. Dash had made love to women before. More than he cared to count. But every one of those women was swept from his mind, their faces, their names, seared away by a fire hotter than any he'd ever known.

Her eyes were dark with an emerald heat; her tangled hair surrounded her head like a fiery aura; her heart hammered beneath his lips. Her ivory flesh gleamed like silk and tasted like temptation. Naked and eager, she was every midnight fantasy come to life, every secret dream fulfilled. And for now, for this one stolen moment, she was his.

Needs drove him to take without patience or tenderness. Emotions were clawing at him, making him forget all about finesse or style. Low, rumbling, inarticulate words were ripped from him—mad curses, impossible promises.

There couldn't be more. For the first time in her life, she was totally, amazingly aware of her body—every nerve, every pulse, every pore. Dizzy from the scent, the touch, the taste of him, Claren clung to Dash, thinking that surely they'd broken all the rules. Passion couldn't possibly get any hotter than this. Or pleasure more intense. But she was mistaken.

When his teeth nipped at the tender white skin at the inside of her thighs, she began to tremble. His mouth was hard and hot and hungry, creating pinpoints of painful pleasure. Drunk with the glory of it, she whispered his name, over and over like a prayer.

Her body was hot and damp and agile as she lifted her hips in instinctive feminine appeal. She'd waited for this all her life. And now finally she was going to experience pure passion.

The blood was pounding in his veins, in his head. Mindlessly he stabbed his tongue into her and heard the strangled gasp of pleasure from her. A gasp that quickly became a moan of need. He felt the sting of her fingernails cutting into the moist flesh of his back, the tightening of her thighs beneath his hands, the tensing of her body as he drove her closer and closer to the brink.

A sulphurous bolt of lightning shot from his lips to some secret, urgent core. Her breath grew shallow, her skin sensitized as that heat gathered, knotted, then exploded, the building flame turning into a sudden flash that raced outward to her fingertips.

Weak, limp, stunned, she was still trying to catch her breath when he surged into her, experiencing a resistance he'd neither expected nor understood. Comprehension dawned with a harsh bright light, but then it was too late. She'd given up her innocence with a soft cry and then she was moving against him, urging him on, racing with him, higher and higher to a place where there was only lightning and thunder. And blinding heat.

IT WAS THE SCENT of her hair—like wildflowers under a summer sun—that brought him back to earth. He was crushing her. Dash felt her lying warm and limp beneath him and felt a despair like nothing he'd ever known.

He rolled off her, cursing himself as he looked down at her face. Her mouth was swollen from his, and a lingering passion clouded her eyes. Under normal conditions he might have experienced male pride for having been responsible for that passion. But these were far from ordinary circumstances.

"Why the hell didn't you tell me?"

Well, they certainly weren't the words of undying love she'd been hoping to hear. Claren, who'd been thinking that now he knew all her secrets, that she'd never be able to hide anything from this man again, slowly opened her eyes. Although she'd been the one to initiate their lovemaking, he'd quickly taken control, tearing down all the barricades she'd spent years erecting, unearthing emotions she'd never dared permit herself to feel.

The dark expression on Dash's face was anything but encouraging. Reminding herself that she'd known from the first what kind of man he was, Claren forced herself to remain calm.

"I didn't think it mattered."

"You didn't think it mattered?" he repeated unbelievingly on a voice that was almost a shout. "You didn't think that a man just might want to know that the woman he's about to practically rape has never been with a man?"

Her aunt had always told her that men preferred virgins. From the tone of his voice, Claren decided that this was yet another thing Aunt Winifred had been mistaken about. Sitting up, she pulled her knees up and wrapped her arms around them. She met his blistering glare with a calm, level look of her own.

"It was far from rape," she reminded him. "Since I was the one who practically attacked you."

Dash was a head taller than Claren, and outweighed her by eighty pounds. That being the case, she damn well couldn't have attacked anyone. "I don't understand. You were engaged. What was Byrd, anyway, a eunuch?"

"Hardly," she reminded him dryly. "He did, however, believe that we should wait to make love until marriage."

"And you went along with that?" Dash stared at her incredulously, wondering how a woman who possessed so much passion could possibly settle for chaste good-night kisses.

"I didn't really want to," she admitted. "But then I didn't really try very hard to change his mind."

Dash wondered about that, but didn't feel up to delving any deeper into the intimate details of Claren's relationship with her former fiancé. "You still should have told me."

"Are you saying that you wouldn't have wanted to make love to me if you'd known I was a virgin?"

"Don't be an idiot." Experiencing that unsettling tenderness once again, he brushed her hair away from her troubled face with fingers that weren't steady. "I've never been known for being very gentle. Or tender. But I would have tried to be. For you."

He frowned as he looked at the darkening bruises on her arms, her legs, her hips. He resisted the urge to kiss the skin his rough beard had irritated. "I would have tried, dammit," he repeated gruffly. "The first time should be special." And damn him to hell, he'd ruined it. Dash wondered if she would ever forgive him for that. And then he wondered, uncomfortably, why he cared.

"It was special. Incredibly so." Reaching up, Claren pressed her fingers against his cheek and gave him a soft, womanly smile that was as old as Eve.

"I never knew," she whispered. "I never knew it could be like this."

For what he'd done, he owed her the truth. "Neither did I." The moment he heard the words come out of his mouth, Dash was ashamed of the hope he saw rising in her soft green eyes. "But as good as it was, it still doesn't change anything. Because I'm no good for you, Irish." There, it had to be said.

"I wouldn't say that."

He hadn't had an easy life, Claren had determined. The lines fanning outward from his eyes, the deep furrow on his brow, the ridges bracketing his mouth attested to experiences both painful and violent. But sometimes, when he let his guard slip, as he'd done a minute ago, she saw a tenderness that assured her that all he needed was time. And love.

Of course he didn't love her. Not yet. But he would. And in the meantime, Claren told herself, refusing to admit that this time she might be biting off more than she could chew, she had more than enough love for both of them.

With an innate sensuality she'd been unaware of possessing, she trailed her hand down his chest, letting her fingers play in the crisp ebony curls. "I think you're very, very good for me."

She flicked at his dark nipple with her fingernail, intrigued by the way it immediately hardened just as hers had under his erotic assault. Claren found the physical response encouraging. It showed that they weren't really so different, after all.

Her teasing touch made his body harden with hunger for her all over again. Dash couldn't think when she was driving him crazy like this. "You don't even know me."

How could he say that after what they'd just shared? "I know you," she insisted softly. "And it's important that you know that I didn't really try to talk Elliott into making love to me because subconsciously I suppose I knew that I didn't really love him. And the reason I wanted you to make love to me—"

"With you," he interrupted, feeling that the difference was important.

Buoyed by the emotion in his voice, Claren nodded her agreement. "The reason I wanted you to make love with me so badly, Dash, is because I love you."

Dash stiffened. He'd known he was making a world-class mistake. Watch the woman, St. John had instructed him. Stay close. Well, he'd watched her all right. For two damn days, even though she'd practically driven him insane with her soft eyes and her hot temper. And he sure as hell couldn't have gotten any closer. So now what was he supposed to do?

"Claren—"

Claren had watched the shock caused by her admission move across his face like an earthquake. Followed by something uncomfortably close to despair. "You don't have to say anything," she said quickly. The color rose in her cheeks again. "I just wanted to tell you."

It was impossible. She didn't know anything about him. She didn't know all the things he'd done. Things he wasn't proud of. Things he couldn't change. Dammit, she didn't know what he was going to do to her.

Dash knew he should say something. Anything. But nothing even remotely suitable came to mind.

Vowing that she'd make him fall in love with her if it was the last thing she did, and wanting to experience the thrill of his lovemaking again, Claren took hold of his hand and tugged him out of bed.

"Let's go try out that wickedly indecent mirrored shower," she suggested. "And we can see how I respond to that tenderness you were talking about."

Dual urges were ripping him apart. He wanted her. He wanted not to hurt her. He retrieved his hand and dropped it to his side. "I can't give you what you want, Claren."

Going up on her toes, she brushed her lips against his. "Want to bet?"

His fingers curved around her waist. Although he knew that he was already in too deep, he found himself pulling her against him. "Darcy told me that you were stubborn."

She smiled against his mouth as she felt his mutinous body respond to her closeness. "Did he, now?"

"He did." Damning himself for a fool and a bastard, he allowed his lips to pluck at hers. "He also told me that you were beautiful."

"My uncle's prejudiced."

"That's what I thought at first. But he was right." His lips skimmed up her cheek to her temple, before pressing against her hair. "You are absolutely lovely."

The low, almost unwilling admission went straight to her heart. Tilting her head back, Claren gave him a smile that lit up her eyes. "What blarney," she said, linking her fingers around his neck. "I love it."

He'd warn her once more, Dash decided. Then it was in her hands. "It's not blarney, Irish. It's the truth. You won't get pretty phrases and soft promises from me."

"I've already figured that out for myself." The laughter in her eyes softened, grew tender. "That's why I intend to cherish whatever wee scrap I get."

God help him, he'd tried. "You're impossible."

"I know."

"You don't have to sound so proud about it."

"But I am. Don't you see, Dash?" she said earnestly. "For years I've tried to do exactly what people expected of me, even though deep inside I knew Darcy was right. I was going against my nature. But finally I've gotten the nerve to break all the rules and I'm having the time of my life."

Feeling absolutely wanton and deliciously sexy, she brushed her body against his. "So, are you coming into that bathroom peacefully, boyo, or am I going to have to use force? Don't forget—"

"I know," he growled as she made his body ache. "The damn judo."

The hell with it. Dash tangled his hands in her hair and gave her a long hard kiss. "You win, Irish," he said, scooping her up in his arms. "But don't say I didn't warn you."

"I won't." She twined her arms around his neck and sighed happily. "Have I told you that I love the way you keep sweeping me off my feet?"

MUCH, MUCH LATER, Claren was sitting across the chipped Formica café table from Dash. After a long, wonderfully fulfilling shower, they'd finally left the horrid, funny room and gone out to breakfast. Starving despite the enormous dinner she'd eaten the previous night, Claren ordered the strawberry whipped-cream waffles while Dash, displaying what she considered a distressing lack of originality, stuck to steak, eggs and cottage-fried potatoes.

She'd learned something important today. Darcy, who'd always had a saying for everything, had told her time and time again that thirst grew the more you drank. Claren had never understood what her uncle had meant until now. Until making love with Dash. Because the more he touched her, the more she wanted to be touched. The more he kissed her, the more she yearned for the taste of his firm lips. And every time he took her soaring to breathless heights she'd never known existed, she couldn't wait to go again.

Thank you, darling Darcy. Even as she acknowledged the painful little hole that Darcy's dying had left
in her heart, Claren couldn't remember when she'd been
so happy.

Dash couldn't remember when he'd felt worse. His
instructions had been specific. He was to get Claren
Wainwright to move into Darcy O'Neill's house by using any ploy he felt necessary. That shouldn't be hard,
St. John had suggested with a knowing leer.

Dash was a professional. One of the best. He had also
gone into this with his eyes wide open. If he had to sleep
with the Wainwright woman to achieve his goals and
to keep from blowing his cover, he would. Such subterfuge came with the territory; it meant nothing.

The hell it didn't.

"It's going to be a beautiful day," Claren said.

Dash glanced out the window. "I suppose so."

She felt like sighing at his unenthusiastic tone, but
didn't. Instead, she smiled at him over the thick white
rim of her coffee mug. "You'll like the festival, Dash."

But his mind wasn't on the festival. "There's something I should have asked you last night."

"What?"

"You are on the Pill, right?"

From his expression, Claren was tempted to lie. But
she couldn't. "Actually, I'm not."

He dragged his hand down his face. "I was afraid of
that." What the hell had gotten into him? He was usually the overly cautious type. But he hadn't even
thought about protection until it was too damn late.

Hating the chasm that was growing between them,
Claren reached out and covered his dark hand with
hers. "I'm sure everything will be okay."

"Yeah." He took a drink of coffee, then eyed her bleakly over the rim of the mug. "I'll bet that's what my mother said in the same circumstances."

Claren refused to let his grim tone burst her little bubble of morning pleasure. "You know," she said, "now that I think about it, I've been rattling on so that you know all about my family. But you haven't said a single word about yours."

"My mother was a seamstress in Guthrie, Oklahoma."

"I envy her," Claren said. "I can't sew a stitch. Aunt Winifred tried to teach me needlework, but I kept pricking my finger on the needle and getting blood all over the white linen pillowcases I was embroidering for my hope chest." Yet another way she'd failed to live up to her aunt's lofty standards, Claren considered. "What about your father?"

"My father was an Indian."

"Really?" Claren surprised Dash with her immediate interest. "How wonderful! And it certainly explains your marvelous cheekbones. I don't know why I didn't realize it sooner. What kind of Indian?"

"A Cheyenne."

"Cheyenne." Claren tried to remember the American history classes she'd taken in high school. "They were a Plains tribe, weren't they? They hunted buffalo and lived in tepees. And they were warriors."

She'd been fascinated by the tales of the Wild West. She recalled the stories of Cheyenne bravery in battle and remembered how sad she'd been at hearing how they'd lost the land they'd loved. Having never stopped missing her own home in County Clare, Claren thought she understood some of what Dash's ancestors must have felt.

"My father was a descendant of Chief Touch the Cloud, one of the tribe's greatest leaders, who died in a battle with the Pawnee," Dash told her. "His people bitterly resented the coming of the white man. The Cheyenne lost more men in fighting than any of the other Plains tribes."

Claren thought back on all the stories her mother and uncle had told her about her own relatives battling the British.

"The O'Neills were persecuted and lost their land," she said softly. "They weren't allowed to practice their religion or speak their language. Just like your father's people." She smiled up at him. "It looks as if you and I have more in common than we thought."

"There's one important difference," Dash said grimly. "My father wasn't married to my mother. He would have married her," he insisted, repeating the words his mother had told him so many times. Words he'd wanted so desperately to believe. "But he was a rodeo rider, and before she got a chance to tell him that she was pregnant, he was killed by a Brahma bull."

"Oh, Dash." Claren's eyes filled with sympathetic tears. "How terrible for your mother."

"She was an incredible woman," he said.

"Was?"

"She died."

"I'm sorry." A tear slid down her cheek; Claren brushed it away.

Dash shrugged. "It was a long time ago. But she sure as hell didn't have it easy, being a single mother in those days, especially when the baby was illegitimate. And although I realize things are different now and people are more accepting, I damn well don't want to be responsible for you getting pregnant like my mom."

His gloomy tone was not encouraging. Claren decided they might as well get everything out in the open. "Have you ever received a Christmas present from someone you hadn't thought to buy one for?"

He wondered at her sudden change in subject but answered anyway. "Sure."

"And did you feel guilty?"

"No." Their last Christmas together, Julia had practically bought out Brooks Brothers in search of the perfect gift for him. Sick and tired of the hypocrisy that their marriage had become, Dash hadn't bothered shopping that year. "All right," he admitted reluctantly, recalling the honest pain in his wife's clear blue eyes, "I suppose I didn't feel real good about it."

"No one does," Claren assured him. "It's always one of the most stressful aspects of the holiday season. I remember one year when I was in college, I had this roommate who I didn't really care for all that much, and she'd never pretended to like me, but then, right before Christmas break, she turned around and bought me a box of almond roca. I felt terrible, because, of course, I hadn't thought to get anything for her."

She was rattling on again, but Dash didn't mind. Because he liked listening to her, whatever she had to say. He turned their hands and linked their fingers together. "Does this story have a point?"

Since he was smiling, Claren didn't take offense at his words. "Actually it does." She took a calming breath and looked him straight in the eye. "When I told you that I love you," she said softly, hurt by the way he inadvertently flinched at the word, "it was a gift, Dash. You don't have to feel guilty if you can't give the same to me."

She looked so sweetly earnest. As he met her warm and loving gaze, the resultant sharp ache nearly rocked him. "Darcy neglected to tell me that you were crazy."

"Crazy about you," she agreed with a grin. "Don't worry about it, Dash," she suggested blithely, cutting into her strawberry-topped waffle, "love's neither contagious nor fatal."

As he returned his attention to his steak and eggs, Dash wished that he could believe her.

THE FESTIVAL WAS HELD atop a bluff overlooking the ferry pier. Laid-back and mellowed out, the people sprawled on the grass and enjoyed the summer sunshine, the music and each other's company.

News of the vandalism at Darcy's house had obviously spread through the small, insular town like wildfire. Dash couldn't count the number of people who came up to Claren and expressed condolences while they examined Dash with unbridled curiosity.

"Maxine and Mildred obviously told everyone about the wedding," Claren said as an aging black musician created magic with the graceful lyricism of his alto sax. "Or lack of a wedding, I suppose, is a better way to put it. So naturally they're all wondering if you had something to do with me calling it off."

"Should we tell them we just met?"

Color flooded her face at the memory of where and how she'd spent the night and much of this morning. Not that she was embarrassed or ashamed, Claren assured herself. It was just that she wasn't ready to have everyone in town know that she'd gone to bed with a man she'd known only two days.

"I don't think that would be a very good idea."

He'd watched the blush stain her cheeks and wondered what a woman who'd displayed the unbridled passion Claren had shown could possibly be embarrassed about. A tall, thin woman started singing along with the sax, her flat tone making Dash wish she wouldn't.

"Whatever you say. I suppose that means you're not going to tell anyone how I kidnapped you, either."

"If I'd had you locked away in jail, I wouldn't have a handyman."

Feeling unreasonably carefree, Dash took her hand and lifted it to his lips. "I knew you were beautiful and sexy, but I hadn't realized you were also practical."

The touch of his lips against her palm made her flesh burn, and Claren found herself wanting him all over again. "If you don't stop that, Dash MacKenzie, I'm going to attack you right here and now."

It sounded eminently appealing to him. He flopped down on his back and spread out his arms and legs in a gesture of surrender. "Have your way with me, Irish. I'm too exhausted from this morning to have the strength to fight back."

He was smiling up at her, and for this brief, shining moment, the harsh lines bracketing his mouth had softened, making him appear much younger and a great deal more carefree than she'd seen him look thus far.

Lying on her stomach beside him, Claren traced the sharp, slanting lines of his cheekbones with her fingers. "That singer sounds as if her shoes are on too tight," she murmured, aware of the strident sound on some distant level as she drank in the rough-hewn features of Dash's face.

"Great minds," he murmured. "I was thinking the same thing."

It was nice, after all the differences she'd detected between her and Dash, to have something else in common, even something as insignificant as an agreement about a singer's talent. She smiled. "You have the most marvelous face," she murmured. "It makes me hope that Darcy's right about my talent. Because I'd love to paint you."

"In the nude."

Her appreciative laughter bubbled free, like a crystal mountain spring. "Of course." The midday sun was warm and soothing. She put her head on his chest, reveled in the feel of his strong arm around her and closed her eyes.

They stayed that way for a long, comfortable time. The sax player and singer left the stage, replaced by a voluptuous woman clad in a rainbow caftan whose amazing, seemingly incandescent voice slid effortlessly up and down a four-octave range as she took one of Louis Armstrong's songs and made it hers. She controlled the beat, turning it inside out, playing it like a yo-yo, never losing it, finally segueing into a long, breathless riff of scat singing.

The woman was the most beguilingly unpredictable singer Claren had ever heard. "She sings like you make love," she murmured as the music rushed through her blood like desire.

"How's that?" Dash sat up and adjusted Claren so she was lying with her head in his lap.

"Her timing is absolutely dizzying. She keeps so many rhythms in the air that when the song is finally over, it's a wrench to have to adjust to ordinary time."

Her words created a burst of male pride. "And that's the way I make you feel?"

She turned her head and smiled up at him. "That's just the beginning. It gets better."

She was the most naturally open person he'd ever met. He wondered how in the hell she'd spent all those years locking those tumultuous emotions inside her. It was a wonder she hadn't gone mad.

"If it's good," he murmured, brushing her tumbled red-gold hair away from her face, "it's not because of me, Irish. It's you."

It wasn't a declaration of undying love. But it was something, Claren decided. And it made her feel wonderful. "Perhaps it's not you or me," she suggested softly. "Perhaps it's us. What we make together."

Dash wondered if there was a man on earth who could resist those expressive green eyes or that soft, ridiculously kissable mouth. "You know, Irish," he said, lowering his lips to hers, not caring who might be watching, "I think you may have just hit on something."

The kiss, because of its public nature, ended far too soon. Lying as she was with her head in his lap, Claren could feel Dash's rising desire, a desire that equaled her own.

She sat up beside him, pulled her knees up to her chest and wrapped her arms around them. "I don't think I had any business lecturing you earlier," she said.

He ran his hand down her hair because he couldn't be this close to her without touching her. "Why?"

"Because I'm suddenly feeling horribly guilty myself."

"What the hell do you have to feel guilty about?"

She sighed and laid her head on her knees. "Darcy's dead and his house is a wreck and all I can think about is that I've never been happier."

Dash wondered how happy Claren would be when she learned the truth. "What's wrong with that?" When she refused to look up at him, he caught her chin between his fingers and gently turned her head.

"Look at me, Claren," he insisted gently, "because this is important." When she met his gaze with suspiciously shiny eyes, Dash continued. "I didn't know Darcy very long, but I do know that all he ever wanted, more than his painting, more than his damn treasure ships, was for you to be happy."

"I really do miss him," she said on a soft catch of breath. "So much."

A single tear trailed down the side of her face. Dash brushed it away with his knuckles. "I know, sweetheart. I miss him, too."

His touch was so gentle, his expression so caring. As she felt that now-familiar speeded-up beat of her heart, Claren vowed that she'd convince Dash that he was a far better, nicer man than he thought himself to be. If it took her the rest of her life.

"Gracious," she said with a nervous laugh and a shake of her head, "I can't believe how I've gotten so maudlin."

"It's probably the music," Dash said. "Jazz has a way of getting under your skin, uncovering emotions you didn't know you had." *The way you do to me.*

"You're probably right," she agreed, eager to grasp on to any excuse. "But if I keep this up, you're going to think all I do is cry." Determined to change the mood before she scared him away, Claren jumped to her feet. "Come on," she said with a dazzling smile that only wobbled slightly, "I'll treat you to a double-scoop ice-cream cone."

Dash wasn't hungry, but he was quickly discovering that he couldn't turn down anything this woman offered. He was walking across the lawn, his hand in hers, enjoying the sunshine, the music and the company, when a movement on the edge of the crowd caught his attention.

He'd seen that guy before, in Jamaica, talking with Darcy. That the man had been angry was obvious; later, when he'd asked Darcy about it, Claren's uncle had brushed the matter off as a little leftover trouble from a recent poker game. But Darcy had been lying. Dash hadn't known why at the time. But he was beginning to get a pretty good idea.

"I think I'd rather go for a drive," he said, quickly turning Claren in the opposite direction before the stranger in question could spot them. "You can play tour guide and show me around the peninsula. I've always wanted to see a rain forest."

He'd seemed to be enjoying himself. Puzzled by his sudden desire to leave the festival, Claren decided not to argue. They would be together; that was all that was important.

As they made their way down the hill, Dash risked a glance over his shoulder. The suspect had been joined by another man. One Dash recognized easily; Interpol had been after him for years, along with the CIA, FBI and similar government agencies all over the world. The man was a terrorist, a professional assassin, infamous for being intelligent, efficient and very, very deadly.

As he practically pushed Claren into the front seat of the rental car, Dash decided that it was probably just as well Darcy had drowned. Because he would have been tempted to kill the old scoundrel himself for putting his only relative, a niece he'd professed to love—a warmhearted, passionate and, most importantly, innocent woman—in harm's way.

9

DASH QUICKLY DISCOVERED the Olympic Peninsula to be a remarkably unruly land. Deep river valleys, tangles of forests and steep alpine mountains seemed designed to frustrate a hurrying traveler. By unspoken agreement, Dash and Claren kept the pace leisurely as they drove on country roads past farms, fish hatcheries and clam and oyster beds, through lush meadows of wildflowers, over crystal streams born in ancient glaciers and beside cool, tumbling waterfalls. It seemed to Dash that there was either a waterfall or a creek around every bend in the road.

When they stopped for a wine tasting at North Mountain Winery, Dash managed to get a call in to St. John, filling him in on the latest development. Then, after a quick check of the winery grounds to make certain that they hadn't been followed, he rejoined Claren, who was waiting by the car with a shopping bag filled with the chardonnay she'd enjoyed, crackers and a variety of cheeses.

"I thought we could have a picnic." She greeted him with a smile bright enough to almost banish the gray clouds gathering overhead.

He looked up at the muted sky. "It looks like rain."

Claren was not to be deterred from her romantic goals. "Fine," she said. "We'll simply have the picnic in the car." Going up on her toes, she pressed her lips against his. The kiss was a flash of heat. "In the back seat."

Despite his lingering concern, Dash smiled. "I think I know how Frankenstein felt when his monster ran amok."

Although he still knew he was making a dangerous mistake, he couldn't deny that making love to Claren was turning out to be the most fulfilling experience of his life.

The Olympic rain forest was a world apart, a land of giants.

"There's no other place in the world," Claren told Dash, "where so many different species of trees grow so tall."

Dash could believe it. Ancient, towering, conifers—spruce, fir and cedar and hemlock—pointed skyward like shaggy dark green arrows, reaching for the bits of sunlight that filtered through the mist and snaggled tree limbs. Mingled amid the conifers were stately hardwoods, their graceful arching boughs upholstered with moss and ferns. Red alders—the youngest of the rain-forest trees—lined the banks of streams.

Myriad other plant forms—lichen, moss, grass and ferns—created a splendid confusion of foliage in countless shades of green. Except for the small dirt trail that had been cut through the lush undergrowth, Dash could not see a single square foot of bare ground. Where the forest floor was too occupied for new growth, plants had adapted by forming a second story: shelflike fungi spread over fallen tree trunks, and trunks and branches of trees were shaggy with streamers of moss. Rotting trees, fallen to the ground, quickly became nurse logs, enabling spruce and hemlock seedlings to sprout from the soon-to-be-vanished log that gave them their start. Wrens hid in the tangled branches of the trees, calling to their mates; beavers and otters made their home in the waters; and flying squirrels glided from tree to tree in the forest canopy.

The moist odor of decay mixed with the crisp scent of conifer needles. Surrounding the shadowy glades was a shimmering luminescence, an amber-green light that bathed everything in its soft, gentle glow.

"I can certainly see why Washington's called the Evergreen State," Dash murmured. "This is remarkable."

"Isn't it?" Claren took encouragement from his uncensored awe and appreciation. Perhaps he'd learn to love this wild, uncivilized land as much as she did. Perhaps enough to want to stay.

"There's something I have to confess," Claren said after they'd left the rain forest. They were sitting on the banks of Lake Crescent; the incredible blue water of the forested lake shimmered in the late-afternoon sun like a star sapphire.

"What's that?"

"I'd much rather be doing this than cleaning up the mess those vandals left behind." She spread some cheese onto a cracker. "Where did you say you found the people who are working while we're having such a wonderful day?"

"Bremerton." He didn't add that the crew was actually from the Puget Sound Naval Shipyard.

"I hope you asked how much they charged," Claren said worriedly.

He ruffled her hair. "Don't worry about it."

"But—"

"I've taken care of it."

"You? But it's my responsibility."

"I know a guy who opened up a janitorial service in Bremerton," Dash said. "He owed me a favor, so I decided to collect."

"That's quite a coincidence," Claren said. It was also a little too pat for comfort.

"Isn't it?" Dash heard the disbelief in Claren's tone and decided the best way to handle it would be to ignore it. "I was planning to drop by and see him after I brought you Darcy's photo album."

There was still something not quite right. Something he wasn't telling her. Refusing to ruin a perfect day with distrust, Claren opted to accept his words at face value. For now. There was, however, one thought that had occurred to her during breakfast. One unpalatable worry that had been nagging at her all afternoon.

"May I ask you something?"

"Sure."

"Are you married?"

Dash let out a slow breath he'd been unaware of holding. Of all the questions he'd been expecting, that wasn't one of them. "No."

"Were you ever?"

"For a while." Dash refilled her wineglass from the bottle they'd cooled in the icy lake water.

"What happened?"

"It didn't work out."

Claren wasn't about to let his curt tone deter her. "Why not?"

"Does it matter?"

"I think it does," Claren answered honestly. She needed to know that Dash had merely chosen the wrong partner, that it wasn't marriage in general that he didn't like.

Dash dragged his hand through his hair, realizing exactly where this questioning was going and why. The woman didn't have a single ounce of guile. He knew he could crush the blatant hope shining in her eyes with the simple truth that he was not the marrying kind. But for some reason, he couldn't do it.

"We wanted different things out of life," he said. "She wanted wealth and comfort." *And a man she could parade around like a trained poodle.*

His answer was not encouraging. But now that she'd gone this far, Claren couldn't back away. "And you didn't?"

"No."

"What did you want?"

Good question. And one he hadn't been able to answer when Julia had asked it of him. "Freedom, I suppose."

"Freedom."

She'd been right all along. He was exactly like Darcy; no woman would ever be able to tie him down. Claren reluctantly accepted the fact that after impulsively diving into uncharted waters, she should not be surprised to discover herself over her head. For now she would try to enjoy herself—and Dash—while she could. There would be times for tears and regrets later.

"We'd better get back," she said, practically jumping to her feet.

He'd watched the vast range of emotions come and go and decided that she may as well be outspoken, because every thought ended up being written across her face in bold script.

"Whatever you say."

A part of her wished that he hadn't been so eager, that he'd suggested booking a room in the nearby lodge. Another part of her wanted to return to Darcy's house, the one place in the world, other than her family's horse farm in County Clare, where she'd always felt safe and secure.

It was dark when they pulled up in front of the house. But the lights had been left on, cutting through the nighttime drizzle with a warm yellow welcome.

As they entered the foyer, both Dash and Claren felt a surge of relief. Dash that St. John's guys were gone, Claren that the house had been put back in such perfect order.

"Your friend certainly works fast," she murmured, roaming from room to room in amazement.

"He always was efficient." That was an understatement. St. John was probably the most thorough man Dash had ever met. Which was why, when he'd insisted the evidence proved Darcy's guilt—and quite possibly Claren's—Dash had reluctantly gone along with his former boss's verdict. In the beginning.

She ran her finger along the top of the mantel, surprised to find not a speck of dust. "He didn't just straighten up the mess. He cleaned, too."

"We'll have to give him a rave recommendation."

"I'll do that," she agreed. "If I knew his name."

From the way Claren was looking at him, Dash knew that she still hadn't quite bought his story. Which wasn't all that surprising since it was so flimsy. He wouldn't have bought it, either.

"I'd better bring in your stuff," he said, sidestepping her pointed remark. "So you can get started painting first thing in the morning. After all," he reminded her before she could utter a single word of objection, "the reason you're here is to explore your talents."

With that he was gone, leaving Claren both curious and frustrated.

Although it took several trips, Dash finally got all Claren's supplies set up in the upstairs bedroom that Darcy had long ago turned into a studio. When she didn't bother to supervise his work, he decided that he'd finally pushed her a little too far. Obviously she was locked away in her room, sulking.

As he went around the house, making certain that all the doors and windows were secured, he considered that Claren was the most frustrating woman he'd ever met. She was also the most desirable. If things had been different . . .

Dash swore, wondering, not for the first time, what was wrong with him. He knew what he was. He'd chosen his life with his eyes wide open. There was no room for regrets, no matter how tempting Claren O'Neill Wainwright might be.

Making love to her had been a mistake. One that wouldn't happen again.

"Sure," he muttered under his breath, "that's why you dropped into the drugstore while she was picking out her brushes and stocked up on condoms."

When Dash walked into his room and found her lying in the middle of the king-size bed, he knew he wasn't going to turn her away. "This is a surprise."

Not exactly a pleasant one, she determined, from the look on his face. "I can leave if you'd rather be alone."

From her tone and the tumultuous emotions he could see in her eyes, Dash knew that she wasn't any more eager to leave than he was to have her leave. To make love to her once—all right, twice, he corrected, thinking back to that wild coupling in the shower—was one thing. After all, they had been all alone in a motel specifically designed for illicit affairs. To take her again now, knowing that he was betraying her trust, would not only be foolhardy, but it would also be impossibly selfish.

The mattress sagged as he sat down on the edge of the bed. "There's nothing I'd like better than to sleep with you," he said truthfully, stroking her fragrant, soft shoulder. She'd showered; the scent of gardenias clung to her silken skin. "But I wouldn't be fair to you if I didn't warn you that this can't go anywhere."

Despite his words of warning, Claren knew that it already had. And heaven help her, although on some distant, reasonable level she knew she was being the biggest fool God had ever plunked down on the planet, she couldn't help wanting whatever Dash was prepared to offer.

Even as she admitted that, Claren realized that some insane part of her actually believed that Dash was falling in love with her. That he was displaying a typical male denseness when it came to intimate matters and simply didn't realize it yet.

She sat up, causing the sheet to fall to her waist, revealing her nudity. "I'm not asking for anything you can't give, Dash," she murmured against his tightly set lips as she linked her arms around his neck. "I'm only asking you to make love with me."

That's what she was saying. But her eyes revealed something else altogether, hinting at a future together that was impossible. Her lips brushed against his, parting invitingly. Her tongue touched his arousingly, making him forget the promises not to repeat this morning's mistake, promises he'd been making himself all day.

When her bare breasts brushed seductively against his chest, Dash was lost. For days he'd thought only of tomorrow. For this one brief moment he was going to give himself permission to think only of today.

"Lord help me, I give up." He took off his clothes, retrieved a foil packet from the pocket of his discarded jeans, tore it open, then joined her in the bed.

"Here," he said, handing her the condom.

"You want me to do it?"

"That's the idea."

Her cheeks flamed. "I don't know how."

"You're a bright woman. You'll figure it out."

Her inexperienced hands fumbled to complete the intimate task, stroking him in a way that nearly made him explode. Dash closed his eyes, gritted his teeth and struggled to remember the starting lineup of the 1964 Yankees.

"There." Claren rocked back on her heels, eyeing her work with a great deal of satisfaction. "That wasn't nearly as hard as I thought."

"Maybe not for you," he muttered as he pulled her astride him. There had been a moment there, between Mantle and Maris, when he'd thought for sure he was going to lose it.

She was ready for him, moist and hot and welcoming. Passion flared in her quickly, as if she'd been waiting for years, rather than a few hours.

Greed overwhelmed, and patience disintegrated. Dash guided the tip of his aroused shaft to that warm, damp place between her thighs, then, cupping his hands around her hips, he surged into her, filling her completely with one long, hard thrust.

"You feel so good," he growled as he felt her body respond to the sudden intrusion. She sheathed him, surrounded him. "Hot and tight and ready for me."

He was deep inside her, stretching her, becoming a part of her. "I've been ready for you for years." The words were torn from Claren in deep gasps. "I've been waiting for you all my life."

There was no gentleness in either of them. Power, heat, desire poured out of him and into her. His eyes remained opened, locked on hers as he allowed her to set the pace and rhythm, a rhythm that matched his own galloping needs. Dash knew that he shouldn't let her race so fast, realized that he should slow her down to allow him to indulge in the leisurely foreplay women preferred. But she felt so damn good.

He took her breast in his ravenous mouth, licking, sucking, biting until her heated flesh was alive with a thousand humming pulses. Her body was slick as she strained against him; her knees pressed tight against his hips; her fingernails dug into his chest as the exquisite, painful pressure built.

Claren clung to Dash as tightly as he clung to her. The breath was trapped in her lungs and her back arched when the coiled spring inside her finally released. A moment later she felt his body tense and heard him shout as he erupted deep inside her. As he shuddered beneath her, Claren couldn't remember when her name had ever sounded so wonderful.

Boneless, she crumpled against Dash, then slowly slid her moist body down him. They lay together in a tangle of arms and legs.

"There's something I have to tell you," Dash said when he could talk again. He was playing with the silky hair that was spread over his bare chest like tongues of flame.

His somber tone was a distinct contrast to the passion they'd just shared. Claren looked up at him, her eyes guarded. "What?" she asked on a shaky whisper. *Please*, she begged silently, *don't tell me that you're leaving. Not yet.*

"I love you." Even as he heard himself saying the unplanned words, Dash knew that they were true. He was also surprised at how good they made him feel. "I love you," he repeated, plucking at the delicate pink lips that had parted on a soft breath of surprised air. Once said, the words came easier with every saying. "Love you."

She could barely believe it. "You don't have to say the words," she said. "I don't need them."

"But I do." She was the purest, most honest person he'd ever met. She was the best thing that had ever happened to him, and although Dash had no idea what he was going to do when the time came to tell her the truth, he did know that he wasn't ever going to let her get away. "You asked me if I was married."

Fear clutched her throat. "And you said you were divorced."

Her flesh, beneath his stroking hand, had turned to ice. "It was the truth," he reassured her. Sitting up against the headboard, he pulled her up with him. "But I want you to know that I never loved my wife. And," he said before she could think him a total jerk, "Julia never loved me."

"You both must have been very sad." Claren, who had nearly married a man she now knew she'd never truly loved, was immensely relieved to have escaped such a terrible fate. She looked up at him, searching for secrets in his hooded eyes. "Why did you marry her?"

"Because she had something I'd always thought I'd wanted."

"What?"

"Wealth and social position in the community."

Claren would have been no more surprised if Dash had suddenly dumped her off the bed onto the floor. "I can't imagine you in society," she murmured.

"Neither could I. Once I got there."

There were so many things about Dash MacKenzie that Claren longed to know. But she didn't want to push him. After all, now that he'd confessed that her feelings weren't one-sided, she'd have the rest of her life to learn all his secrets. The thought filled her with a warm, comfortable glow.

"What about your wife?" she asked. Julia. Dash's wife now had a name. It was a name belonging to a sleek, sophisticated woman. The type of woman she'd tried for so many years to be. "What did she want from you?"

"A trophy," Dash answered unerringly. Julia had been quite honest about her feelings at the time. "A tamed stud she could show off in Park Avenue drawing rooms."

"I can certainly understand that," Claren surprised him by saying.

"You are kidding." He tilted her chin up and looked deep into her eyes. She was the last person he'd expect to have anything in common with his former wife.

"Not really." She pressed her hand against his chest, loving the feel of his heartbeat against her palm. Mine, she thought wonderingly. He's all mine. Dash MacKenzie was more than her lover; he was her destiny. "If you want to know the unvarnished truth, Dash," she said, "I rather liked showing you off at the jazz festival today."

"Did you, now?"

"I'm afraid I did. Especially after what Maxine had said about Elliott."

Even the sound of the guy's name was enough to send a jolt of jealousy through Dash. Reminding himself that the former groom-to-be hadn't even managed to take Claren to bed, Dash forced down the hot, uncharacteristic emotion. "What did she say?"

"Say?" she asked idly as her fingers played with the crisp dark hairs covering his chest, following the arrowing over his stomach.

"Claren." Sounding half-strangled, Dash grasped hold of her hand just as it ventured into forbidden territory. "What did Maxine say about Byrd?"

"Oh, that." She was entranced by the way Dash's body was already revealing that he wanted her again. As she wanted him. "She told me that everyone in town had been worried about his apparent lack of masculinity."

"They actually discussed that?" Dash had almost forgotten how gossip provided the mother lode of entertainment in small towns. His parents had certainly borne the brunt of it enough times. As had he.

"Apparently in great length," Claren agreed, unaware of the sudden tensing of Dash's jaw. Her attention was currently directed to other parts of his body. "It seemed several people were worried that Elliott wouldn't be able to satisfy me. Sexually or emotionally."

Tugging her hand loose of his light hold, she wrapped her fingers around his burgeoning length. "But you needn't worry, Dash," she murmured throatily. Her breath stirred in the crisp dark hair between his tight thighs, making him rock hard. "No one could ever say that about you."

When her lips caressed him in the most intimate kiss of all, Dash sucked in a deep, painful breath. "Dammit, Irish," he groaned even as he lifted himself into the willing warmth of her mouth. She'd been a virgin only a few short hours ago. So how the hell had she learned to drive him over the brink? "You're going to drive me crazy."

She certainly hoped so. Claren had been working on instinct alone, but from his agonized response she realized that she was definitely on the right track. How strange that there were so many books written on the subject of sex, she mused as she caressed the buttery soft male flesh with her lips, her tongue. When all she had to do was to follow her heart.

Just when he thought he was going to blow sky-high, Dash grabbed hold of her tangled hair and lifted her head. "One of these days," he said tightly, struggling for control, "if and when I can ever think coherently again, remind me to tell you that you are incredible."

With hands that were not as steady as he would have liked, he quickly sheathed himself, then, unable to wait another minute, he rolled her over on her back and buried himself in her silken warmth. The storm of release broke quickly, leaving them both shuddering. And hurling Dash into a deep intimate relationship that a mere two days ago he'd neither expected nor wanted.

OVER THE NEXT WEEK, they fell into a predictable routine. After breakfast Dash worked on all the projects that had been put off too long, and Claren would go upstairs, where she'd spend the morning in her studio. They'd break for lunch, and more often than not, make love before going back to work. Evenings they spent in front of the fire, sharing what they'd both done that day. When the flames had burned down, they'd go upstairs to Dash's wide bed.

Immersed in the pleasure of newly discovered love and the agony of artistic creation, Claren failed to notice that Dash disappeared several times during the day. She did, however, notice that he seemed to be growing increasingly edgy.

"You're getting ready to leave, aren't you?" she asked on the morning of their eighth day together.

Dash looked up from his waffles. "Of course not. Whatever gave you that idea?"

"You've been acting just like Darcy," she said. "Whenever he was about to take off on another expedition."

"I'm not Darcy," Dash pointed out. "And I'm not going anywhere."

"Then why—"

Dash was relieved when the intercom at the gate buzzed, cutting off her questioning.

"Hello?" Claren answered.

"Claren? It's me. Elliott."

"Go away."

There was a moment's shocked hesitation. "Claren, please, I just want to talk to you."

"We have nothing left to say to one another."

"I'm not leaving here until we talk. Come on, Claren, you're not being fair."

Claren exchanged a look with Dash, who shrugged, letting her know the decision was totally hers. "Come on up to the house," she decided on a sigh. "But I'm very busy, so I can only give you five minutes to say whatever it is you came to say."

"Thank you, darling," he said, sounding more humble than she'd ever heard him.

Less than three minutes later the doorbell rang. While Claren went to answer it, Dash drank his coffee and asked himself how could he tell her that the reason for his edginess was that the two men who had quite possibly come to Port Vancouver to kill Claren had disappeared so efficiently that even St. John, with all his worldwide contacts, hadn't been able to learn their location.

Waiting had always made him edgy, but now that Claren was the target, Dash had been going quietly out of his mind.

"Hello, Elliott," he heard Claren say. "This is certainly unexpected."

"I brought your clothes," Elliott Byrd offered. "Your aunt thought you might want them."

Claren thought about all those dreary little business suits in the gloomy colors and wondered what had ever possessed her to buy them in the first place. "That's very considerate of Aunt Winifred," she said, "but she really needn't have bothered. Why don't you take them back and give them to the Salvation Army?"

"Give away perfectly good clothing?" Elliott looked at Claren as if she'd grown an extra head. "What will you wear to work?"

"In case you've forgotten, Elliott," Claren responded coolly, "I quit my job. At your request."

"Of course I remember." He ran his long, delicate fingers through his thin blond hair. "But I assumed, after you came to your senses, that you'd be returning to Seattle."

"For your information, I have come to my senses, Elliott."

"I'm relieved to hear that. We've been quite concerned."

"Interesting how none of you have called to see how I was doing."

A red flush rose from his collar. "Actually I was away, but I assumed your aunt would have telephoned."

"Away?" She wondered if he'd been so humiliated by her behavior that he'd felt it necessary to leave town until the gossip died down. "Where did you go?"

"Hawaii."

"Hawaii?" Claren stared at him in disbelief. "You went on our honeymoon by yourself?"

"Actually I didn't go by myself." The red flush staining his face darkened. "Lisa went with me."

"Lisa? My maid of honor?"

"Well, all the arrangements were made for two," Elliott answered defensively. "It seemed wasteful not to use the extra ticket."

"Or the honeymoon suite?"

"It could have been you, Claren."

"Thank God it wasn't," she responded hotly.

"If you're still angry about the paternity suit—"

"I'm not angry about the damn lawsuit!"

"You don't have to shout, Claren."

"I'm not shouting," she yelled. "You still don't understand, do you? What made me furious was the fact that you lied to me."

"I didn't lie. I never told you I could have children."

"It was a lie of omission," Claren countered. "You knew I wanted a large family and you just let me rattle on, picking out names, talking about how wonderful it was going to be, and all the time you'd already made certain that we wouldn't have any children."

"I was going to tell you."

"When?"

"When it was appropriate."

"When it was too late for me to do anything about it," she countered hotly.

"Claren." Elliott put his hands on her shoulders. "It would have worked out," he insisted, tightening his grip when she tried to shrug it off. "You know as well as I do that our careers, not to mention my political future, would not have left any time for a child. We were going to have such a good life, darling," he said, pulling her toward him. "We still can. If you'd just stop being so stubborn."

Claren glared up at him, wondering how she'd ever thought she'd been in love with this man. "You lied to me, Elliott."

"I didn't mean to hurt you." He massaged her tense muscles. "It's not too late." He lowered his head. "I think I made a crucial mistake not making love to you," he said. "It would have created a bond between us."

Claren couldn't believe it. "You want to make love to me? Now? After everything you've done?"

His lips were a whisper from hers. "We can put that in the past, Claren." He drew her closer. "Trust me."

Dash decided that he'd heard enough. "The lady would do better to trust a boa constrictor," he growled as he entered the entrance hall.

Elliott looked up in surprise. "Who's this, Claren?"

"I'm the man Claren's going to marry," Dash heard himself say. As surprised as he was to have made such a statement, he immediately found it eminently satisfying. "I'm also a very jealous man, Byrd," he warned on a soft, deadly voice. "So if you know what's good for you, you'll take your hands off my woman."

"Your woman?" Elliott dropped his hands to his sides and backed up, his startled gaze darting from Dash to Claren, to Dash, then back to Claren. "This is your way of paying me back," he finally decided. "You want me to think that you have something going with this guy."

Claren's mind was still whirling from Dash's stunning pronouncement. But not so much that she couldn't enjoy Elliott's obvious discomfort. "Actually, I do have something going with Dash," she said, going to stand beside him. "He's my lover."

"Your lover?" Elliott's pale blue eyes widened farther.

"Her lover," Dash confirmed. Putting his arm around Claren, he hauled her against him.

"I don't believe it."

Rather than answer, Dash lowered his head and captured Claren's unresisting mouth. As always heat instantly flared, making Claren forget that this kiss was supposed to be for show. She went up on her toes and threw her arms around the strong dark column of Dash's neck. Her avid mouth clung to Dash's in a way that could never be feigned.

Dammit, she was doing it to him again. The way her hungry little mouth was eating into his was making Dash hard. Forcing down his desire for now, he broke the heated contact and eyed her former fiancé over her head.

"Believe it," he advised.

"Claren," Elliott said, obviously shaken, "I can understand why you'd want to have an affair in order to pay me back for some perceived indiscretions. But I can't allow you to marry this obvious Neanderthal."

"You don't have anything to say about it," Dash said before Claren had a chance to open her mouth. "You gave up all rights to Claren when you chose to betray her. So you may as well go back to Seattle, Byrd. Because there isn't anything for you here."

A muscle jerked in Elliott's finely sculptured cheek. "My mother was right all along," he said acidly, giving Claren a sharp, censorious look. "Blood *will* tell. It's obvious that you're just as irresponsible as your dead uncle. As for your lover," he said, shooting Dash a glowering glance, "I wouldn't be at all surprised to discover a few scalp hunters in his family closet."

That said, he turned on his heel and marched out of the house, slamming the carved oak door behind him.

"Dash?" She'd felt him stiffen at Elliott's scathing accusation. "Are you all right?"

"Yeah." He forced himself to relax—neck, shoulders, arms. "How could you let yourself get mixed up with a creep like that?" The words had been familiar, as had the superior disdain. They'd been as much a part of his growing up as the beatings.

"I don't know. I suppose it's proof of how truly lonely I was," Claren said on a sigh. "But I don't want to talk about Elliott. He's in the past, and I have every intention of keeping him there."

She twined her arms around his neck. "As for the present and the immediate future, how about going upstairs and letting me ravish you?"

"That sounds immensely promising." Pushing down all the logical reasons why this could turn out to be the mistake of a lifetime, Dash lifted her into his arms and carried her up the curving stairway to the bedroom.

10

"THAT WAS WONDERFUL," Claren murmured.

"It always is." Dash ran his hand down her side from her shoulder to her thigh, loving the silken feel of her still-warm skin beneath his fingertips.

"I wasn't talking about that," she said. "Although you're right, it was terrific. Every time we make love, it's like the first time. Only better."

She smiled up at him and pressed her lips against his. "However, I was referring to the way you let Elliott think we were getting married. Although I detest lies, I have to admit that one definitely hit its mark. I can't ever remember seeing him so shaken."

"I wasn't lying."

"What?"

"I said," Dash repeated slowly, enjoying the wealth of emotions flooding into those incredible green eyes, "I wasn't lying. I want to marry you, Claren. If you'll have me."

"If I'll have you?" Joy bubbled up like water from a sparkling stream. "I thought you'd never ask."

Dash's expression was not that of a man who'd just proposed marriage. Instead, he looked like a prisoner on the way to the gallows. "Before you give me your answer, there are things you need to know. Things about me."

"I love you." Claren took his hand and linked their fingers together. "That's all I need to know."

She was too damn trusting. Dash was forced to wonder, not for the first time, if Darcy had used his niece's trust to involve her in his deadly scheme.

Forcing that distasteful thought aside, he said, "I told you about my mother not being married."

"Surely you don't think that would bother me?"

"No. It's just that I don't know exactly where to start trying to explain about me. About who I was."

"The beginning isn't such a bad place," Claren advised, confident that there wasn't anything Dash could tell her that could change her mind about him.

"My mother was the only person, besides you, who ever loved me," he began, feeling more nervous than he'd ever been in his life. "She died when I was five."

"Oh, Dash," she repeated, past the lump in her throat. "I'm so sorry."

He lifted their joined hands to his lips and kissed her fingertips. "When I first met you, I realized that you were probably one of the few people in the world who could understand the way I felt the first morning I woke up and she wasn't there."

How strange that it was their shared tragedy that had provided the bond that made Dash fall in love with her, Claren mused. Once again she couldn't dismiss the idea of destiny.

"She was soft and gentle, but so frail," Dash said on a low, flat tone. "I was with her at the end. I held her hand and begged her not to leave. But she did."

And he'd been suffering the loss ever since, Claren decided, her heart aching for the five-year-old boy Dash had been. "What happened to you?"

"I spent the next few years in foster homes," he said. There was an edge to his voice that Claren had learned to recognize. "It wasn't easy. In those days, in Oklahoma, I was considered a half-breed because of my Cheyenne father, so I ended up being shunned by both races. I suppose some kids would've been beaten down, but I fought back. I wasn't exactly a model kid.

"In fact, I was in and out of the juvenile detention center so many times that eventually the state ran out of foster homes willing to take me. So when I was ten, I landed in the Oklahoma Bible Fellowship home for wayward boys."

The tears were flowing unabated down Claren's cheeks. At thirteen, living in her comfortable luxury of her aunt and uncle's home, she'd thought her life unbearable. She'd been oblivious to exactly how terrible life could be for other, less fortunate orphans.

"The guy that ran the place was a hellfire-and-brimstone preacher," Dash said. "His idea of the perfect way to end the day was ten lashes with his leather belt."

"He beat you?"

"The way he looked at it, it was his duty to save our souls, and if we hadn't done something that day, we sure as hell would the next."

"I can't believe the state would license such a home."

Dash shrugged. He'd put those days behind him long ago. "The boys that ended up there were considered destined for prison. I think the state had pretty much given up on rehabilitating any of us."

"But you didn't end up in prison."

"No. I was one of the lucky ones," he said, thinking back on how he'd run away at fourteen. And how St. John had subsequently saved his life.

"I don't think it was luck," Claren said. "I think it was courage."

Despite her wobbly smile, a single tear remained on her cheek, glistening like a diamond. Dash brushed it away with his knuckle.

"I love you," he murmured with a certain hint of wonder. "So much."

Claren smiled. "That's good." She kissed him briefly before gathering up her clothing. "I don't believe in marriages without love. And now for the true test." Her voice was muffled from the canary-yellow T-shirt she'd pulled over her head.

"What test?"

Her head emerged, her flame hair tousled like a gypsy's. "I'm going to see how honest you are."

A fist gripped his gut. "What are you talking about?"

Distracted by trying to turn her white jeans rightside out, Claren didn't hear the tension in his voice. "I'm going to show you my paintings. And I want you to promise that you won't say anything you don't mean."

Ten minutes later Dash was standing with Claren in her studio. She'd shown him canvas after canvas and was now waiting for his opinion.

"They didn't teach art criticism in the home," he hedged.

"I'm not asking for an expert opinion, Dash," Claren insisted. "I just want to know what you think. It's important to me."

He stood in front of an abstract oil. "I like the colors," he said, looking at the bold slashes of blue and green and red that reminded him of crayons. "And there's certainly a great deal of energy." That much was definitely true; the paint seemed to almost leap from the canvas.

"You don't like it."

"I didn't say that."

"I know, you like the colors. And the energy. But what is it?"

She had him there. "I don't know," Dash admitted reluctantly. "But that doesn't mean anything," he hastened to add. "I've never understood abstract art."

"It's the jazz festival."

"Of course it is. I don't know why I didn't see it right away."

"Because it isn't any good," Claren said, unable to lie to herself. "I don't think abstract is my style. What do you think of my watercolor landscape?"

Once again the colors were crayon bright, rather than the soft, washed hue he was used to seeing in watercolor. At least this he could recognize as the rain forest. "It's certainly bright."

"Too bright," Claren agreed. "And the perspective is all wrong. So much for landscapes." Stifling a sigh, she pulled another canvas from behind the watercolor. "It's a portrait of you. But I got the eyes all wrong. And the cleft in your chin looks as deep as the Grand Canyon, and one ear is higher than the other. I may as well face it," she muttered, "Darcy was wrong. I don't have any talent."

Dash hated seeing her so depressed. Although he was no expert, the one thing all three paintings had in common was their passion, the same passion Claren had revealed in bed.

"Perhaps some lessons," he suggested carefully.

"Lessons may help the problem with my perspective," she said. "But they can't change the way I feel." She slumped down on a nearby chair. "I hate painting."

"But you've been locked away in here for a week. And every time I asked how it was going, you said you were having a wonderful time."

"I lied."

He arched a black brow. "Claren O'Neill Wainwright, model of veracity, lie?"

"Don't tease me, Dash," Claren begged. "It's just that I wanted so badly to change my life. I didn't want to have to go back to Seattle and rejoin the rat race. I wanted to stay here," she said on something close to a wail, "like Darcy wanted, in this wonderful house and utilize my talent."

"Perhaps you still can." An idea had been playing at the back of his mind; now seemed like the perfect time to bring it up.

"I love the fact that you're so supportive, Dash," Claren said. "But you don't have to worry about my feelings. I know that I'm never going to be a painter."

"Perhaps your uncle was talking about another talent."

"What? I sing off-key and am totally tone-deaf. As for writing, I can whip off a pretty fair memo, but when it comes to fiction or poetry or anything creative, I'm an absolute dud, which is terribly depressing, considering that Ireland is renowned for its writers.

"I can't dance, I've never twirled a baton and the one time I was in a play at school I got stage fright and forgot my lines. All two of them."

"Claren, Claren." Hating to see her so distressed, Dash drew her into his arms. "This isn't the end of the world."

"Maybe not for you," she mumbled into his shirt, "but I feel like an absolute failure."

"You're far from a failure, sweetheart," he soothed, stroking her back comfortingly.

"Oh, I know I'm good in bed," Claren sniffled with the absolute lack of guile he'd come to expect from her. "But that's just because you're such a good teacher," she wailed.

"It's because you've got the instincts of a courtesan," he corrected. "But that's beside the point, for now. I was referring to another talent."

Claren looked up at him through misty eyes. "What talent?"

"Running a hotel."

"I know I can do that," she said, not bothering to hide her exasperation. How could he not understand? "But I told you, Dash, I don't want to go back to Seattle."

"So don't go."

"Fine. Shall you call the Whitfield Palace and inform them that from now on I'll be performing my duties long-distance or shall I?"

"I'm not talking about the Whitfield Palace. I'm suggesting that you scale back and do what made you go into the hotel business in the first place."

"Run a bed and breakfast in Ireland?"

"Perhaps you don't have to travel that far. Didn't you tell me that before Darcy bought this place, it was—"

"An inn," she said, wondering why such an incredibly perfect idea hadn't occurred to her during all those long, lonely, frustrating hours slapping paint onto canvases. "You're right." She beamed. "It's such a perfect solution, Dash. And I'm good at my work, really I am."

"I haven't a single doubt of that."

"I'll have to come up with a brochure," she said. "And prices. And every room in the place is going to need a major overhaul, and there should be flowers. Acres and acres of them, enough so that there can be fresh blooms in every room every day. And..."

Her voice suddenly dropped off as an unpalatable thought forced its way through her elation. "I didn't even ask if you'd hate the idea of living in a hotel."

"If I hated the idea, I wouldn't have brought it up. And it certainly sounds as if you're going to be in the market for a handyman."

"You'd do that? For me?"

"For us," he corrected. "After I ran away from the home, I met this guy who made furniture for a hobby. He let me move in with him and taught me everything I know." A faint smile hovered at the corner of Dash's harshly cut lips as he thought back to those days in St. John's basement. "Until you put me to work, I'd forgotten how much I'd enjoyed working with my hands."

Claren knew that she'd never—in her entire life—been happier than she was at this moment. "Speaking of working with your hands..." She began unbuttoning his shirt.

"My God, woman, you ever get enough?"

"Of you?" Claren pressed her lips against his chest and imagined she could actually taste the warm, sexy, speeded-up beat of his heart. "Never." She pushed the denim work shirt off his shoulders, allowing it to fall to the floor.

When she began to unsnap his low-slung jeans, Dash captured her hands. "Not here."

"Yes." She had a sudden urge to have him take her here, on the floor in the slanting warm sunshine. "Please, Dash."

Her green eyes were filled with myriad sensual invitations. Her hands fluttered against his chest like delicate birds. "I love you, Irish," Dash said softly, firmly. "Enough to take care of you."

She knew immediately what he meant. Unfortunately she hadn't thought to stash condoms in every room of the house. "But it isn't necessary, Dash. I love you. And I want to have your baby."

"I want that, too, sweetheart," Dash assured her, marveling at how his life had changed in a little more than a week. There'd been a time when he would have rather been hung by his heels over a tank of piranha than settle down and father children.

But that had been before Claren. Dash knew that whatever happened between them, from now on life would be divided into two periods: Before Claren and After Claren.

"But as much as I'm looking forward to being a father," Dash said, "I'm not going to be responsible for bringing a bastard into the world. I know firsthand how hard that can be on a kid."

"But our child wouldn't be illegitimate," Claren argued. "Because we're going to be married."

"That's what my parents thought, too," Dash reminded her. "But it sure as hell didn't work out that way, did it?"

Looking a long, long way up, she saw the rigid determination on his face and inwardly sighed. The one thing Claren had learned during their time together was that there was no point in arguing with Dash when his eyes turned to flint the way they were now.

"We're not your parents," she reminded him softly. "Life is too messy and far too random to keep repeating itself through successive generations. I feel so positive about us, Dash. I just know that we're going to have a wonderful life together and people will come from all over the country—the world—to stay at the picturesque little inn on the Olympic Peninsula run by that friendly couple."

She framed his frowning face between her palms. "And although they'll have a wonderful time, years from now guests will leave just a little scandalized at the way two people in their nineties still lust after each other the way we will."

That idea, Dash had to admit, was eminently satisfying. "You've got it all planned, don't you?"

"Not really. All I know is that I love you and you love me and that's all that matters."

Was it, though? Dash wondered. What would happen to her love when she discovered he'd been deceiving her from the beginning?

"Come on," he said, linking their hands together, "if we're going to be a scandalous couple in our old age, we'd better start practicing."

"Darcy always said that practice makes perfect," Claren agreed happily as they walked hand in hand down the hall, back to the bedroom.

CLAREN HAD never been happier. Having abandoned her futile effort toward a career in art, she threw herself into the refurbishing of the inn with a fervor like nothing Dash had ever seen.

"You remind me of the Tasmanian Devil," he said late one afternoon. She was sitting on the floor of the dining room, fabric samples strewn over the parquet floor, strips of floral, striped and paisley wallpaper tacked to the wall.

Claren glanced up, amazed as always at how just looking at him could cause her heart to triple its beat. "Who?"

"You know, the Tasmanian Devil. The cartoon character," he said at her blank look. "Kind of a whirling dervish."

"Oh. Aunt Winifred didn't approve of cartoons."

From what Dash had learned of Claren's aunt, it was obvious that there was very little the woman did approve of. For not the first time since he'd met Claren, he was forced to consider that although she'd lived in the lap of luxury, emotionally she'd been every bit as deprived and lonely as he had been.

"I was trying to suggest that you've been working too hard," Dash said.

"But there's so much to be done," Claren protested. "Most of the wallpaper's dreadfully faded, and did you notice that there's a water spot on the ceiling of the Mt. Rainier Room? I'm certain the roof must be leaking. And the carpets need cleaning, and the floors need to be stripped and waxed, and the woodwork definitely needs painting, not to mention—"

"Claren. Sweetheart." Dash caught her hands in midgesture. "Back when your aunt was teaching you all those Bible quotes, did she ever have you read Ecclesiastes?"

"Of course, but what does that have to do with leaky roofs?"

"It states," Dash reminded her, "that there's a time for every purpose under heaven. A time to be born, a time to love, a time to put new shingles on the roof and a time to go dancing."

"You want to go dancing?"

"The wooden-boat festival dance is tonight," he reminded her. "I want to show you off."

"That sounds horribly chauvinistic."

"Perhaps. But I still want to hold you in my arms in front of the entire town and stake my claim."

"More chauvinism," Claren pointed out on an exaggerated sigh. "Whatever am I going to do with you?"

He pulled her to him for a long, hard, wonderful kiss. "Ask me that later tonight, sweetheart," he said when they finally came up for air, "and I'm sure I'll be able to come up with plenty of ideas.

"But first I have something I want you to wear tonight. For me." Reaching into his pocket, he pulled out a small black velvet box and put it in her hand.

"Oh, Dash." Claren's eyes misted over as she opened the box and viewed the sparkling green tourmaline set in gold. "It's beautiful. But can you afford it?"

He'd been living on expenses for years, while his salary had been accumulating in various bank accounts, but not knowing how to explain that to Claren, he simply said, "The jeweler gave me a good deal."

Relieved that he hadn't gone into debt on her account, Claren smiled up at him. "I love it."

"I know a diamond's more traditional." Incredibly nervous, Dash felt like a kid on his first date. "But I saw this stone in the window and it reminded me of your eyes, so I couldn't resist. But we can take it back and exchange it if you want."

"Never." She picked the ring from its velvet bed and held it out to him. "Please, put it on."

A painful lump rose in his throat as he slipped the ring on her outstretched finger. "Let's get married now," he said, suddenly terrified that he'd lose her. "Tonight. Before you change your mind."

Claren would have laughed were it not for Dash's frighteningly serious expression. "I'm not going to change my mind," she assured him. "You're stuck with me, Dash MacKenzie. For the rest of your life." She brushed her lips against his, slowly, seductively, causing flames to rise and burn away his lingering fears. Almost.

The heated kiss was interrupted by the sudden peal of the doorbell. "Let's pretend we're not home," Claren murmured against Dash's lips.

But whoever was outside was not prepared to give up easily. The bell rang again. A third time. "I'd better go see who it is," Claren said reluctantly.

She stood in the doorway, staring at the enormous crate. "This can't be for me. You must have the wrong address."

"You Claren Wainwright?" the deliveryman asked.

"Yes, but—"

"Then I've got the right place." He turned the clipboard so she wouldn't have to read upside down. "Claren Wainwright, 1256 Mountainview Road, Port Vancouver, Washington. U.S.A. This is yours, lady."

"I'm Claren Wainwright," she agreed. "And you have the right address, but I'm not expecting anything this large." Her eyes narrowed as they took in the wooden crate. "What is it, anyway?"

Khaki brown shoulders lifted in an uncaring shrug. "How should I know? I just deliver the stuff. Look, lady," he said, casting an impatient look at his watch, "I've still got a lot of stops to make today. So why don't you just sign on this line, right next to your name, so I can get back to work, okay?"

Claren ignored the outstretched plastic ballpoint pen. "But I didn't order anything."

"So maybe somebody sent you a present. Please, lady," he begged, "just sign the damn delivery slip."

"I've got one question," Dash said, surprising Claren, who hadn't heard him come up behind her.

"Not you, too," the heavyset man groaned. "I don't know what's in the damn crate."

"That wasn't my question."

"Sorry." To Claren's amazement the deliveryman suddenly snapped to attention at Dash's rigid tone. She would not have been at all surprised if he'd saluted. "What can I do for you, sir?"

"How did you get through the gate?"

"Simple. I just got out of the truck, opened it and drove through."

The answer was enough to make the hairs on the back of Dash's neck stand on end. "It wasn't locked?"

"Nope. I mean, no, sir."

Dash handed Claren a pen from his pocket. "Why don't you sign the delivery slip, darling," he said with a great deal more calm than he was feeling. "So the man can continue his route."

Claren was about to argue that this was all a mistake when she saw something alien flash in Dash's eyes. If she hadn't known better, she would have thought it was fear. Which was, of course, impossible, she decided as she reluctantly scribbled her name. Dash was the bravest man she'd ever met.

"Where do you want it?" the man asked.

Before Claren could answer, Dash said, "Out in the yard."

It obviously wasn't the answer the deliveryman was expecting. "It's pretty heavy," he pointed out. "You sure you don't want me to haul it inside for you?"

"The yard is fine," Dash repeated.

Again those broad khaki shoulders shrugged. "Hey, it's your crate." He backed down the steps, rolled the crate out onto the yard and tipped it carefully off the hand truck. Then, with a muttered curse after looking at his watch, he ran back to the brown delivery truck. With a roar of the engine and a cloud of black exhaust, he was gone.

"Well," Claren said, circling the crate, "it can't be an early wedding present, because nobody knows we're getting married yet. Except Elliott," she amended. "But I don't think he'd send us a present. Unless he could figure out a way to make it explode," she tacked on, remembering the look on his face as he'd slammed out of the house.

Explosions were exactly what Dash was worried about. Until he noticed the date the package had been shipped. The day before Darcy's death.

"Why don't you go upstairs and start getting ready for the dance," he suggested, "while I find a hammer and uncrate this."

"Are you kidding?" Claren asked. "Now that I'm stuck with this thing, I'm dying to find out what's in it."

So was he. Half expecting a treasure trove of plundered booty from the *Maria Theresa*, Dash didn't know what to make of the contents of the crate.

There appeared to be nothing of value, merely items designed to appeal to the tourist trade. There was a grass skirt out of ti leaves that Dash decided would look more than a little appealing on Claren, a coconut carved to look like a monkey's face, various clay figures, colorful baskets and numerous strings of beads created from pink and white shells.

"Gracious," Claren murmured, staring at the figure of an obviously pregnant female, "she's certainly, uh, robust, isn't she?"

"She is that," Dash murmured, running his hand over the molded clay, searching for seams. The statue's round breasts and distended belly had been exaggerated, designed to represent the female in her most fundamental form. "I suppose, considering your desire to give birth to your own basketball team, we can consider this a wedding present from your uncle."

Claren found the sight of Dash's dark hand moving over the statue's swollen breasts painfully erotic. What was happening to her? Ever since she'd met the man, she'd had sex on the brain.

"Darcy always sent me gifts from his travels," Claren agreed. "But never anything so . . ."

"Erotic," Dash finished up when her voice seemed to fail her. "She reminds me of you."

"Of me?" Claren's hands went immediately to her flat stomach; for some strange reason she could not comprehend, she almost expected to find it large with child. "That's the way you see me?"

"Not physically," he assured her. "But emotionally. She's all woman, round and soft and made for having babies. Just like you."

"That's not exactly a flattering description, Dash," Claren felt obliged to point out. "Sometimes, when you talk like that, I get the distinct impression that you're not really a modern man of the nineties."

"If you're referring to the egocentric kind of guy who sleeps around on his fiancée and fixes it so she can't have the children she's always wanted, I guess I'm not."

"Thank heavens." Claren smiled up at him. "I've come to the conclusion that I much prefer a more primitive man."

Dash lifted a challenging dark brow. "Primitive? Like in Neanderthal?"

"Primitive like in old-fashioned," she corrected. "In a good sort of way." She twined her arms around his neck. "You really meant it, didn't you?" she asked. "What you said that first morning about protecting me."

"I'd protect you with my life," Dash agreed roughly, hauling her to him. With a burst of passion that surprised them both, he covered her smiling mouth with his.

The kiss rocked her. Dash didn't ask; he took. Although she never would have thought it possible, it was more thrilling than any of the others they'd shared so far. Claren clung to him, as if only he could keep her from spinning off the edge of the world. His mouth was urgent, restless, moving over her face from her lips to her temples to her chin, as if wanting to taste all of her at once.

Tongues met, his teeth nipped at her lower lip and she would have been afraid of the strength of such unchecked passion if she hadn't been so in love with him. Her mind spun and she recalled his reference to Ecclesiastes and she knew that this was a time for feeling, for giving freely. There would be time to think later. For now she wrapped her arms around him and gave unconditionally.

"I want you to promise me something," he said, his lips a hot breeze against her temple.

"Anything," Claren answered breathlessly, meaning it.

He tangled his fingers in her hair and tilted her tawny head back so he could look directly into her eyes. "This is important," he insisted on a voice that was not as steady as it should have been. "I want you to promise that whatever happens between us, you'll never forget that I love you more than I ever thought possible."

His face could have been cut from granite, and something Claren could not quite discern blazed in the gleaming pewter depths of his eyes. Whatever it was, it frightened her.

She lifted her palm to his cheek; the muscle jerked beneath her stroking fingertips. "You make it sound as if we're about to be visited by plague and pestilence," she whispered in an attempt at levity that fell decidedly flat.

He turned his head and capturing her hand in his, pressed his lips against the tender skin of her palm, causing her pulse to leap. "Promise me," he insisted.

Her knees were shaking, her lips were trembling. Never, even when they'd been making love, had Claren felt such passion emanating from his tense body. "I promise."

He'd needed desperately to hear the words, but now that she had, he realized he needed more. Much, much more. What he needed, dammit, was for all this to be over.

Releasing her so quickly that she almost fell down, he picked up the statue, lifted it over his head and, ignoring Claren's cry, flung it to the ground. The clay cracked apart, leaving another statue, shaped exactly like the first, but formed from gleaming gold.

"Oh, my God." Claren knelt down and ran her hands over the gold surface. "How did you know?"

"It's a fairly standard practice," Dash said. "For smugglers."

She looked up at him, clearly startled. "Are you accusing Darcy of being a smuggler?"

"I'm not accusing him of anything."

But his eyes were saying something entirely different. Stunned that Dash could believe something so hateful about the only other man she'd ever loved, Claren couldn't bear to look at him.

"I'm going upstairs to get ready," she said. "Before I say something I'll regret and call you a liar."

With that threat ringing ominously in his ears, Claren left Dash alone with the grinning gold statue. He tapped the rotund figure, unsurprised by the hollow tone.

"Cute, Darcy," he muttered. "Real cute." He took the statue with him into the house and called St. John.

"I've got your damn goddess," he said. "You can come take it off my hands while we're in town tonight. It'll be in the library in O'Neill's secret hiding place in the bookshelf, behind Arthur Conan Doyle. And, St. John? This is the last job I do for you."

He smiled grimly as the smooth, round tones on the other end of the line began the expected argument.

"I mean it," he said. "Tomorrow morning I'm starting a new life with the woman I love. And although I know it's going to break your heart, there isn't any place in it for you."

The only father figure he had ever known was still arguing when Dash hung up the receiver.

11

THEY WERE, unsurprisingly, the talk of the town. Claren, dressed in a backless flowered sundress, flitted around Pioneer Hall, showing off her ring to everyone. That she was loved was obvious, which was why, Dash decided, the citizens of Port Vancouver had accepted him so readily.

Already he'd received three invitations to go flyfishing, two more invitations to go backpacking on Hurricane Ridge and several other requests for his assistance in various environmentalist movements designed to protect the peninsula against encroaching development from the Puget Sound cities.

A drummer from the Port Vancouver jazz society wanted to know if he played an instrument and Helen Riddenour, a zaftig woman with a remarkably deep voice who owned a local gallery, asked if he had any talent for wood carving, since native American art sold wonderfully well to eastern tourists. Not wanting to offend the woman, Dash was trying to get away gracefully when Claren suddenly appeared beside him.

"Darling," she said, flashing a sweetly apologetic glance Helen Riddenour's way, "you promised you'd dance the next slow dance with me. You'll excuse me, won't you, Helen?" she asked as she practically dragged Dash onto the dance floor.

"Remind me to thank you for rescuing me when we get home," Dash murmured as he gathered Claren into his arms.

The hand holding hers was strong and hard, with a ridge of calluses from the hard physical work he'd been doing. "Helen's always been a bit pushy." His arms fit around her perfectly, and he was incredibly light on his feet for such a large man. And Claren couldn't believe how handsome he looked in the unfamiliar blue suit.

"She thought I might be able to supply her with some native American art."

Claren tilted her head back and looked up at him, searching for hurt in his eyes. "What did you say?"

"Don't worry, Irish, I didn't embarrass you. In fact, I was incredibly polite, although I was tempted to point out that my ancestors were too busy scalping her ancestors to worry about carving pretty knickknacks."

Claren couldn't miss the tinge of bitterness in his tone. "You don't ever have to worry about embarrassing me," she insisted loyally. "But I am sorry about what Helen said."

He shrugged. "She was just looking for a quick commission."

"Does it bother you?" she asked quietly. "That your father was an Indian?"

"Hell, no," Dash said quickly. "I'm proud of my heritage, Claren. Does it bother you that our children will be one-quarter Cheyenne? That our sons and daughters will have warrior blood flowing through their veins?"

"Of course not. I only worried that Helen might have hurt your feelings."

"I'm a lot tougher than that, Irish." Dash pressed a kiss against her fragrant hair. "What does grate is people like your former fiancé, people who wear their prejudice like a badge of honor."

He tipped her head back with a finger beneath her chin and brushed his lips against hers. "But that's enough angry talk for the evening. I just want to hold you in my arms and thank whatever fates or gods sent you to me."

The words, and the emotion behind them, came as a surprise. Dash was not a man for poetry or pretty phrases. He'd warned her about that from the beginning. Claren had quickly discovered that whatever Dash said, he meant. He was not a liar, like Elliott. He was the most honest man she'd ever met. And the nicest. And the sexiest. And—

"What are you thinking?"

She smiled up at him. "How much I love you."

His arms tightened as he practically crushed her against him. "I hope you always will."

He could be so intense sometimes! Claren assured herself that his seeming desperation was only the result of an overactive imagination and the two glasses of wine she'd drunk.

"Of course I will." Going up on her toes, she kissed him, oblivious to the amused glances of the other couples on the dance floor. "Forever and ever," she promised as the music stopped and the band announced that they were taking a fifteen-minute break.

They were headed off the dance floor when Dash saw St. John appear in the doorway and gesture toward him. Furious at the interruption, he said, "I'll be right back." When Claren glanced up at him curiously, he added one more lie to the growing string he'd already told her. "Nature calls. That's what I get for drinking that second beer."

A soft color flooded her cheeks; her only response was a brief nod.

It had gotten warm in the hall. When Dash didn't immediately return, Claren decided to slip outside for some fresh air. The redbrick building was located on the waterfront and, drawn by the site of the bright lights on Discovery Bay, she strolled idly down to the ferry dock and watched the large white boat's approach.

"You found me," she said with a smile, turning around when she heard the footfalls behind her. "I was worried—"

Her words were cut off as she was roughly grabbed from behind. A hand clamped over her mouth, forestalling any attempt to scream. Claren struggled to strike out at her assailant, but he was much larger and a great deal stronger.

"Damn you, bitch," he muttered when she slammed her high heel down on his foot. "You'll pay for this." He put his forearm against her neck and squeezed, causing spots to swim in front of her eyes. She was nearly overcome by vertigo; her lids fluttered closed.

"Don't kill her," another voice, with a vaguely European accent, instructed sharply.

"I'll second that," a third man said. Claren's eyes flew open at the wonderfully familiar sound of Dash's deep voice. He was standing in the shadows; the steel of the pistol in his hand gleamed silver in the moonlight. "Let her go."

"Why the hell should we do that?" Yet another man wearing a black turtleneck sweater and black slacks emerged from the shadows, his pistol pointed at Dash. "When there are three of us and one of you. And we've got your girlfriend."

"I'm giving you one last opportunity to change your mind," Dash said. Claren found his cold tone to be amazingly calm and incredibly reasonable, considering the highly unreasonable circumstances. It was almost as if he were accustomed to such potential violence. "Release Ms. Wainwright now, or you'll live to regret it."

The arm around Claren's midriff tightened, making breathing difficult. When she felt the cold blade of a knife pressed against her throat, ice skimmed up her spine.

"I wouldn't try anything," her captor warned. "Unless you want to see the bitch's throat cut."

Rage surged through Dash, but he forced it down. He took a deep breath, encouraging his mind and his body to relax. It was a technique he'd learned from a Buddhist monk in Tibet and it was working. A deep calm spread over him like a comforting quilt; all his senses were intensified.

"Just give us the goddess," the second man said reasonably. "And we'll let the woman go. There's no reason for her to end up like her uncle."

"My uncle?" Claren stared at him. "You killed Darcy?"

"He knew too much," the man answered reasonably, as if he were discussing the weather or the Seattle Seahawks' chances for a winning season, rather than cold-blooded murder. "We scuttled our boat when we learned that the authorities were searching for it. Your uncle stumbled across it in his treasure hunt and unfortunately for him, he proved too nosy for his own good."

Claren didn't have the faintest idea what Dash was going to do to extricate them from this situation, but she had no doubt that he would. Trusting him implicitly, she decided to try to buy as much time as she could while hopefully distracting her uncle's killers.

"What was on the boat?" she asked. "Drugs?"

"Emeralds," the man who appeared to be the spokesman for the unholy trio answered. "They were on their way to Miami, where they'd be handed over to a local businessman whose expertise is dealing in hot gemstones."

Claren suspected that he wouldn't be telling her all this if he planned to keep his word and let her live. But she also knew that Dash would never let these men kill her.

"So you killed Darcy for money?"

"Money's simply a tool. A tool used to buy revolution," he told her. "Those emeralds are going to pay for a lot of sophisticated weaponry on the arms black market. Which is why," he said, an impatient tone creeping into his voice, "we must insist you give them back."

"But I don't have any emeralds."

"Don't try to lie. We know you received a package from your late uncle. The emeralds are inside the smaller of the two fertility goddesses. We put it inside the larger one to double our protection in case something happened to prevent our man in Miami from pulling the shipment before it went through customs. So, I'm going to ask you one more time. Where is she?"

"I don't know what you're talking about."

The man made a clucking sound with his tongue. "Didn't your mother ever teach you that nice little girls don't lie?" he murmured in a low, deadly tone. "Perhaps you need a little persuasion." He nodded at her captor. Claren felt the knife blade nick her skin, drawing blood.

At that moment, an elderly woman stumbled into their midst. "Excuse me, but is this the ferry pier? Gracious," she gasped, putting a white-gloved hand to her mouth. "I seem to have interrupted something."

"Get the hell out of here, you old bag," the man ground out. "Before you end up feeding the fish in the bay."

"Feeding the fish," the old woman repeated. "Why, isn't that a delightfully colorful phrase. A bit clichéd, perhaps, but ..."

Instead of finishing her sentence, she lowered her curly gray head and plowed into the man's midriff. Caught off guard, he crumpled to the wooden deck. At that same instant Dash kicked out, knocking the knife from Claren's assailant's hand. It went skittering across the planks and beyond, sinking into the cold dark water. Dash's fist sent the man sprawling to the deck beside his companion.

The third man in the deadly trio grabbed hold of Claren and held her in front of him as a shield.

"Back off," he warned Dash, "and she won't get hurt."

Fed up with the way these horrid men were ruining what should have been the most romantic evening of her life, Claren shifted her weight and took a deep breath. An instant later there was a surprised shout as the man holding her landed on his back on the pier with a thud.

"Good God," Dash muttered, staring down at Claren's supine victim. "You really do know judo."

"I told you I did," Claren reminded him. "You should know by now that I never lie."

"Speaking of lies—" Dash began.

"Excellent." A deep voice cut off his planned confession. Claren spun around to stare at the newcomer. "You haven't lost your timing MacKenzie," he said. "And I confess that I'm quite impressed with your martial-arts skills, Ms. Wainwright," he added to Claren.

"As for you—" he strode up to the elderly lady and yanked her silvered hair "—I'd say it's about time to rejoin the living."

"Uncle Darcy?" Claren stared at her uncle, who was dressed in a print dress with a lace collar, heavy support stockings and white orthopedic shoes. "You're alive!"

"No thanks to these hooligans," Darcy said, glaring down at the three men sprawled on the ground. "They did their best to kill me, but they didn't know old Darcy O'Neill's like a cat. I've got nine lives." Appearing undaunted by Claren's obvious shock, he turned to Dash. "I knew you'd take care of my girl."

"What?" Claren's shocked gaze went from her resurrected uncle to Dash. "Did you know about this?"

"I honestly believed Darcy was dead."

But now, faced with the elderly man's disguise, he realized he'd seen Claren's uncle before. The first time had been in the Pelican's Roost, the first night he'd arrived on the peninsula with Claren. The second occasion had been at the Timberline; at the time he hadn't paid proper attention to the elderly woman engaged in conversation with the bartender. Darcy had obviously been in Port Vancouver the entire time.

"Damn," he muttered. "I should have figured it out."

"You weren't looking for an old woman," Darcy pointed out. "It was a perfect disguise. Those thugs even walked right past me at the jazz festival and didn't look twice."

"It's my job to see things others don't," Dash said.

Comprehension slowly dawned. A cold black shadow moved across Claren's heart. "You knew about the goddess all along, didn't you, Dash?"

He dragged his hand down his face. "Yes."

"And that's why you came to Port Vancouver. To get her."

"It was more than that," the man who'd applauded Dash on his fighting skills answered. "Peter St. John, at your service, Ms. Wainwright." He waved his arm, and a quartet of beefy men suddenly appeared to whisk Claren's attackers away with an air of efficiency that suggested foiling murder attempts were all in a day's work.

"After Darcy was seen diving near where the smuggler's boat had gone down," St. John continued, "we thought he might be part of the terrorist cell we'd been keeping under surveillance for the past year."

"That was a damn coincidence," Darcy interrupted hotly. "I was looking for the *Maria Theresa* when I came across the scuttled boat. I was going to write her off as just another hurricane victim when these gangsters started threatening me, warning me that I'd be a dead man if I went anywhere near her. Well, naturally that piqued my interest."

"Of course," Claren muttered. There were times—
and this was definitely one of them—when she thought
that her uncle's emotional and mental growth had
ceased at the age of twelve. "So, unable to resist the lure
of smuggled treasure, you dove down again. And that's
when you found the goddess."

"Located her during a night dive," Darcy agreed with
remarkable cheerfulness. "I boxed her up along with
some other knickknacks and sent her to you, wrote out
a will and had Dash witness it, then went back down.
Those hoodlums had vandalized my oxygen tank,
leaving me with only ten minutes of air."

He grinned. "What they didn't know was that I'd already stashed a spare tank near their boat."

"But why?" Claren asked. "Why did you feel you had
to fake your death? Do you have any idea how horri-
ble I felt? I cried for you, Darcy. Buckets and buckets
of tears. I honestly thought I'd lost the only person who
loved me. How could you do such a terrible thing to
me?"

"I was truly sorry about that, darlin' Claren," Darcy
insisted. "But it wasn't as if I had much of a choice. After all, it was as clear as the nose on this old Irish face
that those cutthroats had marked me for death as soon
as I ran across their treasure. I had to throw them off
the track, don't you see?"

He gave her a conciliatory smile. "But I was worried
that they'd come after you, so I fixed things so that Dash
would watch out for you, even if he did think you and
I were in cahoots with the terrorists."

Claren spun toward Dash, her eyes filled with an-
guish. "You thought I was a criminal?"

"No. Never." Dash raked his hands through his hair and decided he'd told his last lie. "All right, in the beginning I thought that there was an outside chance that Darcy had involved you in something illegal. But after I met you, I realized that you definitely weren't terrorist material."

"Actually that's the truth," St. John confirmed. "Soon after he arrived here on the peninsula, Dash began insisting that you weren't involved in the scheme."

"You've no idea how that relieves me," Claren said dryly. Her head was aching and her heart felt as if it had an enormous hole in it. "Who are you, really?" she demanded of Dash. "And what are you?"

Dash felt like reminding her that he was the man who loved her. But from the look on her face, he knew that she wouldn't buy that. Not now. Not after all that had happened.

"My name really is Dashiell MacKenzie," he said. "And I used to work for NIS. But I retired nearly four years ago."

"NIS?"

"Naval Investigative Service," St. John answered for Dash. "Our jurisdiction is to investigate crimes on naval bases, along with those committed on the high seas. We also get involved in counterintelligence, which was Dash's area of expertise. He was one of our top agents."

"Was?" Claren asked.

"I told you," Dash insisted, "I retired."

"I can vouch for that," Darcy said. "When I first met Dash, he was the head of security for his father-in-law's international construction company."

"What are you talking about?" Dash demanded, clearly surprised by the statement. "I never laid eyes on you until you showed up on the island."

"That's true enough," Darcy agreed. "But I certainly laid eyes on you. Your wife had dragged you to a gallery opening in Soho. As luck would have it, a friend of mine, Colin Kavanaugh, owned that gallery, and since I happened to be in New York at the time, I dropped in for a bit of champagne and some conversation about art. That's when I saw you, leaning against a far wall, arms crossed over your massive chest, looking frightfully bored.

"Well, of course I wanted to know right away who that glowering giant was," Darcy continued. "I had it in my mind to paint you, you see. Do you know that you have the most marvelous face? It's the face of the quintessential warrior. And those savage cheekbones—"

"Why don't you just get on with the story?" Dash growled.

"Well, Colin filled me in on both your marriage and your job. Along with the interesting tidbit of gossip that you'd been rumored to have done some not very nice things during your time at NIS."

"So," Darcy said with a bold leprechaun's grin, "when I got in my little difficulty on the island, I knew you were the man for the job. And this proves I was right, too," he said. "Isn't fate a marvelous thing? To think that we both ended up on the same island at the same time. Remarkable."

Fate, Claren thought. She'd once thought that fate had brought Dash into her life. Her destiny, she'd called him. She dragged a trembling hand through her hair.

"You came here to spy on me."

Dash felt as if the sky had fallen on him. "Maybe I did. In the beginning. But once I got to know you, I knew there was no way you could be guilty, Claren," he insisted. "You have to believe that."

"Why should I believe anything you say?" she asked heatedly. "When so much of what you told me, from the beginning, was nothing but lies."

"Not all of it."

He moved toward her, but she backed away, holding her hands up in front of her as if to ward off contamination. "I'm going back to the dance," she said. "And I'm asking Maxine to take me home with her. When I return to the house tomorrow, I expect to find every trace of you gone.

"As for you," she said, turning toward her uncle, "we're going to have a long talk."

"If it's about the house," Darcy said, "I want you to keep it, darlin'. I heard you, back at the dance, talking about your plans for turning it into an inn and I think that's a splendid idea. So long as you keep my studio vacant," he added as an afterthought.

"I don't believe any of this," Claren muttered.

She turned and walked away with an amazing amount of dignity for someone whose life had just been destroyed.

She'd almost reached the hall when a hand reached out of the shadows and snagged her arm, hauling her against a hard, rigid body.

"Dammit, Dash!" Her struggles were useless; he was much stronger and, it appeared, even more determined than she. "Let me go!"

"Not until we talk." Throwing her over his shoulder the way he had the night of the vandalism, he strode down the street, mindless of the crowd that had come out of the hall to watch.

"You're creating a scene. People will think you're a bully. And a brute."

"You should know by now that I don't give a damn about what people think about me." Except for Claren, Dash amended silently. About her feelings, he cared a great deal.

"I'll scream," she warned heatedly.

"Go ahead and scream that gorgeous red head off," he invited. "But it won't stop me."

Instead of turning toward the parking lot as she'd thought he would, Dash began walking along the waterfront. "Where are you going?"

"Somewhere we can talk undisturbed."

"If you think there's anything you can say that will make me forgive you, you're sorely mistaken, Dashiell MacKenzie. It would be easier for a herd of camels to spit through the eye of a needle!"

Appearing unperturbed by her threats, Dash walked into the sheriff's office as if he owned it. If the woman behind the desk was surprised to see him carrying Claren over his shoulder like a sack of flour, she didn't reveal it. When Dash pulled out his wallet and displayed his NIS identification, she swiftly snapped to attention.

"If you wouldn't mind, Sheriff," Dash said politely, "I'd like to commandeer your facilities. To interrogate my prisoner."

"Of course." She stood up from behind the desk, took her hat from a peg on the wall and walked to the door.

"Molly," Claren protested, "how can you leave me alone with this man? I insist you arrest him for kidnapping. Right now."

"Sorry, Claren," the sheriff said, "but federal authority supercedes local jurisdiction. Good luck," she said, winking at Dash.

"Oh, Claren," she said, turning in the doorway, "I heard about your engagement. Congratulations. I know Dash will make a much better husband than that lily-livered Byrd fella. I'll be back in the morning. If you're still here, we'll have breakfast."

"It is absolutely disgusting," Claren said through clenched teeth, "the way women fall all over themselves to oblige you."

"Not all women," he pointed out. "You've driven me crazy from the moment we met."

"And you've lied to me from the moment we met," Claren countered hotly. "So I guess that makes us even."

"Not yet." He reached into a desk drawer, found the ring of keys, then, shifting her to the other shoulder, carried her into the back of the building.

"What do you think you're doing?" Claren yelled as she viewed the barred cells.

"We need to talk. Somewhere we won't be interrupted and some place you won't be able to run away." Dash opened the door to the first cell, carried her inside, then closed the barred door behind him.

"You were right about me being a throwback to another time," he informed her mildly. "I'm a hell of a lot more possessive about my woman than modern guys like Byrd. If you think I'm going to let you hightail it out of here, the way you ran away from your wedding, you have a great deal to learn about me, Irish."

After making certain the door was secured, he tossed the key through the bars. It bounced against the wall and landed a good five feet from the cell.

"I can't believe you did that."

"Believe it." Dash tossed her lightly on the cot, then sat down beside her. "Now, you can go ahead and get it out of your system."

"Get what out of my system?"

"All that bottled-up anger. I probably deserve it."

"Probably?" Her voice and her temper rose. "You lied to me, Dash."

"Would you have let me stay with you if I'd told you the truth? That I'd come to Port Vancouver because certain highly placed individuals in the government thought that your uncle might have joined a bunch of terrorists in his old age? And that those same individuals considered you a suspect, too?"

"I don't know. Probably not," Claren admitted. "But the ends don't justify the means."

"I was going to tell you."

"Oh?" She arched an argumentative brow. "When?"

"Tomorrow." It was the truth. After having his recently discovered conscience keep him awake too many nights in a row, he'd decided to disregard his orders and tell Claren everything. At least all that he'd known.

"Tomorrow. How convenient. And why am I supposed to believe you?"

"Because it's the truth. Dammit, it is," he insisted furiously at her challenging look. "I've been wanting to tell you everything, but St. John didn't want to play it that way."

"And St. John is your boss?"

"Former boss," Dash corrected. "He and I go back a long way. Remember me telling you how I used to get in a lot of trouble when I was a kid?"

"I remember." Claren folded her arms over the front of her sundress. "I suppose you're going to tell me that was another lie?"

"It was the truth. After I ran away from the home, I bummed around a lot, hitchhiking from state to state. When I was fifteen, I stole a Corvette in D.C. It turned out that the car belonged to St. John. He was navy brass, assigned to the Pentagon at the time.

"For some reason I'll never understand, instead of having the cops throw the book at me, he took me into his home, made me go back to school, arranged for me to go to the naval academy, then brought me into NIS.

"I worked in counterintelligence for eight years and yes, I did some things I'm not very proud of. But they seemed necessary at the time. When I discovered that the once unthinkable was in danger of becoming the routine, I got out.

"I was sitting on the beach, minding my own business, trying to decide what I was going to do with the rest of my life, when your crazy uncle showed up and got himself killed. Or at least I believed he was dead," Dash amended. "The next thing I knew St. John's men were climbing all over the island, furious as hell because Darcy had landed himself in the middle of their damn black program and—"

"Wait a minute," Claren broke in. "A black program? I don't understand. What does some type of civil-rights legislation have to do with terrorists?"

"You're thinking of a program for blacks," Dash corrected. "A black program is one that's kept off the books when it's time for congressional funding."

"Because it's illegal?"

Dash winced, recalling how minor nuances such as legality and morality had once seemed nothing more than an irritating deterrent to his work.

"Not exactly. And before you get up on your high horse, I didn't want anything to do with this entire operation. I was sick of playing James Bond. But then I started thinking about Darcy and what a nice old guy he'd seemed to be and how he'd obviously adored you and before I knew it, I was volunteering to come here and keep an eye on you."

"Because you thought I was a terrorist."

"I didn't think you were a terrorist, dammit!" Dash roared. "From the moment I met you, I realized that you were about as benign as Mary Poppins."

"I'm not certain I should take that as a compliment."

"I meant it as one."

"You said you got sick of playing spy. Is that why you went to work for your wife's father?"

Her voice was cooler than he'd heard it. And unnaturally calm. Dash worried that she'd already shut her heart to him.

"Partially. But she wasn't my wife at the time. I'd been working for Warren Van Pelt for about six months when Julia came back from Europe to lick her wounds after a particularly messy divorce.

"She saw me as a challenge and a trophy. After the men of her social set, stuffy, predictable guys like Byrd, she found me an interesting specimen."

"She actually said that? In that way?"

"Actually that was one of the nicer descriptions she used," he allowed. "By the time we got a divorce, she was opting for much harsher terms." He shrugged. "Some of which I probably deserved. It didn't take long for both of us to realize that I didn't belong in her world any more than I belonged in her father's rigid corporate structure. Julia and I stuck it out for three years before finally calling it quits. That's when I went to Jamaica...."

"But I don't want to talk about my marriage," he said. "I brought you here to talk about us."

"I don't know," Claren mused. "If you're trying to prove that you've mellowed since your marriage, Dash, I don't think locking me up in a jail cell is the way to do it."

"The only thing I'm trying to prove is that I love you, dammit!" Dash roared again, frustration eating away at the ragged edges of his self-control.

"By holding me hostage?"

"If that's what it takes, yes."

Claren was furious at him for lying to her, for pretending to be something he wasn't, for tossing her into this cell and literally throwing away the key. But she also loved him. Whoever he was, whatever he'd done.

"I suppose I can't say you didn't warn me," she murmured, thinking back on all the reasons he'd given why they shouldn't become lovers, all the ways he was wrong for her.

"I knew that first time I kissed you, in the library, that it was already too late for warnings," he said.

"Too late for me? Because you realized I was falling in love with you?"

"Too late for you, too late for me. Too late for both of us." His voice had dropped to the lower registers, to that deep, husky tone that never failed to thrill her. "I think I fell in love with you the moment I saw you marching down that road with your veil flying out behind you and your satin train dragging in the dirt."

"I was so upset," she said softly. "And you wouldn't leave me alone."

"I couldn't. For numerous reasons, the least of which concerned St. John and that damn goddess."

Sensing her surrender, he put his arms around her and drew her close. At first she stiffened, but then, as he ran his hand down her hair, she began to relax.

"I came here to do a job, Claren. And I kept trying to convince myself that's the only reason I was staying, even though I think I knew from the beginning that you were a great deal more than an assignment.

"I also tried to tell myself that I had good reasons for lying to you, Irish. And to tell you the truth, I'd probably do it all over again if I thought it would keep you safe. But I never lied about my feelings or my background or the fact that I want nothing more than to spend the rest of my life making mad passionate love—and babies—with you."

Claren decided that she couldn't demand total honesty from Dash without being honest herself. "Speaking of babies," she said softly, "I think we've already got a head start."

His startled gaze dropped to her still-flat stomach. "Are you sure? How—"

"I'm pretty sure," Claren said. "At least, if you can believe the test kit I bought at the drugstore this morning. As for how, I assume in the usual way."

"But when?" He'd been so careful, except for that first morning. "Oh, God, please don't tell me that we made our baby in that ridiculous adult motel."

Claren's smug, womanly smile reminded Dash of the Mona Lisa. "I'm afraid so. Which means we both have to swear never to let the truth come out. Can you imagine growing up with the knowledge that you'd been conceived in a heart-shaped water bed?"

She was having his child. Fate, Dash decided, was a remarkable thing. "I've done nothing in my life to deserve you," he said, his voice husky with emotion. "But if you're still in the market for a husband handyman for your inn and a father for our child, I'd like to apply for the job."

"Back there, on the pier," she said quietly, gesturing to the ferry landing next door, "I wanted to hate you. I wanted to hurt you and I think I even wanted you to crawl after me on your hands and knees."

"If that's all it takes—"

"No." Claren's lips curved in a faint smile. "You don't have to get down on your knees, Dash. Because the absolutely frightening truth is that I love you and I want to spend the rest of my life with you. To work with you and have your babies and sit beside you on the porch in our rocking chairs, watching our twenty-five grandchildren play tag on the lawn in front of the inn."

Dash lifted a brow. "Twenty-five?"

"Well, if we're going to have five children, and each of them has another five—"

"I get the idea." Pulling her against him, he kissed her, his lips creating sparks from one smiling corner of her mouth to the other. It was going to be all right. They were going to be all right.

"There's something I was going to give you," Dash said. "After I'd come clean about everything." He reached into his suit pocket and pulled out a pair of red, white and blue envelopes.

"Airline tickets? To Ireland?"

"For our honeymoon. There's something else." He took another slip of paper from the same pocket.

"It's a bill of sale," Claren said on a sharp indrawn breath.

"For a certain horse farm in County Clare."

"Please Dash," she begged, unable to read the print because of the tears filling her eyes, "don't tease me. Not about this."

"I wouldn't do that. I've talked with the couple currently living in your old house by phone a few times, and they seem like nice folks. I think you'll like them. They've agreed to stay on as caretakers. If you want, we can move there—"

"No." Her head was spinning. So much had happened in the past hour. Her beloved Darcy was alive, Dash was a spy and she'd finally gotten her old home—her parents' home—back again. "I want our children to grow up Americans," she said. "But I want them to love Ireland, too."

"We'll take lots of vacations."

"I don't know how to thank you, Dash," Claren said breathlessly. "This means all the world to me."

"I'd give you the world if I could."

And he would, too, Claren knew. He'd take it apart and put it together any way she wanted, if only to make her happy.

"I don't want the world, Dash. I only want you. So why don't you take the spare key out of your pocket and unlock the door like the clever ex-spy I fell in love with and we'll go home and make up properly."

Her lips were sweet and tender, her body was practically melting against him and Dash felt his own desire rising to new heights. But there was one small problem.

"Uh, Claren . . ."

"Mmm?" She was nibbling on his earlobe.

"I'm afraid you kind of threw me off track at the pier and I made a major miscalculation."

She looked up at him with laughing eyes. "Dash MacKenzie, master spy, doesn't have another key?"

"Afraid not."

"Well, then," she said on a slow, seductive smile. "I suppose we'll just have to think up a way to pass the time until Molly comes back in the morning. Any ideas?"

"How about I hold you in protective custody?"

"My hero." Claren sighed dramatically as he purposefully pressed her down against the mattress of the narrow cot.

That was all either of them was to say for a very long time.

A Note from JoAnn Ross

I've always been a sucker for reluctant heroes—men like Sydney Carton, the drunk, dissipated lawyer who, because of his devotion to Lucie Darnay, takes her husband's place at the guillotine in *A Tale of Two Cities*.

Or war profiteer Rhett Butler, kissing Scarlett while Atlanta burned, then heading off for what he knows is a lost cause.

And, of course, cynical, mysterious Rick of *Casablanca* fame, giving up Ingrid Bergman in an act of pure heroic selflessness.

Reluctant heroes are surly, sarcastic, often downright rude. They're lonely men, men who have suffered, men who have opted out of life. But they all possess a steely inner core of integrity they ultimately can't ignore.

Romance with a reluctant hero never runs smoothly. A woman brave enough to love such a man must be intelligent, resourceful, spirited enough to stand up to him and patient enough to prove to him that he's better than he thinks he is.

She must tempt and torment even as she teaches him to trust. Until finally, after struggling with the dark pain of his past, the reluctant romantic hero like Dash MacKenzie learns to put his faith in a bright future with the woman he loves.

OFFICIAL RULES • MILLION DOLLAR WISHBOOK SWEEPSTAKES
NO PURCHASE OR OBLIGATION NECESSARY TO ENTER

To enter, follow the directions published. If the Wishbook Game Card is missing, hand-print your name and address on a 3″ ×5″ card and mail to either: Harlequin Wishbook, 3010 Walden Ave., P.O. Box 1867, Buffalo, NY 14269-1867, or Harlequin Wishbook, P.O. Box 609, Fort Erie, Ontario L2A 5X3, and upon receipt of your entry we will assign you Sweepstakes numbers (Limit: one entry per envelope). For eligibility, entries must be received no later than March 31, 1994 and be sent via 1st-class mail. No liability is assumed for printing errors or lost, late or misdirected entries.

To determine winners, the Sweepstakes numbers on submitted entries will be compared against a list of randomly, pre-selected prizewinning numbers. In the event all prizes are not claimed via the return of prizewinning numbers, random drawings will be held from among all other entries received to award unclaimed prizes.

Prizewinners will be determined no later than May 30, 1994. Selection of winning numbers and random drawings are under the supervision of D.L. Blair, Inc., an independent judging organization whose decisions are final. One prize to a family or organization. No substitution will be made for any prize, except as offered. Taxes and duties on all prizes are the sole responsibility of winners. Winners will be notified by mail. Chances of winning are determined by the number of entries distributed and received.

Sweepstakes open to persons 18 years of age or older, except employees and immediate family members of Torstar Corporation, D.L. Blair, Inc., their affiliates, subsidiaries and all other agencies, entities and persons connected with the use, marketing or conduct of this Sweepstakes. All applicable laws and regulations apply. Sweepstakes offer void wherever prohibited by law. Any litigation within the province of Quebec respecting the conduct and awarding of a prize in this Sweepstakes must be submitted to the Régies des Loteries et Courses du Quebec. In order to win a prize, residents of Canada will be required to correctly answer a time-limited arithmetical skill-testing question. Values of all prizes are in U.S. currency.

Winners of major prizes will be obligated to sign and return an affidavit of eligibility and release of liability within 30 days of notification. In the event of non-compliance within this time period, prize may be awarded to an alternate winner. Any prize or prize notification returned as undeliverable will result in the awarding of the prize to an alternate winner. By acceptance of their prize, winners consent to use of their names, photographs or other likenesses for purposes of advertising, trade and promotion on behalf of Torstar Corporation without further compensation, unless prohibited by law.

This Sweepstakes is presented by Torstar Corporation, its subsidiaries and affiliates in conjunction with book, merchandise and/or product offerings. Prizes are as follows: Grand Prize—$1,000,000 (payable at $33,333.33 a year for 30 years). First through Sixth Prizes may be presented in different creative executions, each with the following approximate values: First Prize—$35,000; Second Prize—$10,000; 2 Third Prizes—$5,000 each; 5 Fourth Prizes—$1,000 each; 10 Fifth Prizes—$250 each; 1,000 Sixth Prizes—$100 each. Prizewinners will have the opportunity of selecting any prize offered for that level. A travel-prize option if offered and selected by winner, must be completed within 12 months of selection and is subject to hotel and flight accommodations availability. Torstar Corporation may present this Sweepstakes utilizing names other than Million Dollar Sweepstakes. For a current list of all prize options offered within prize levels and all names the Sweepstakes may utilize, send a self-addressed stamped envelope (WA residents need not affix return postage) to: Million Dollar Sweepstakes Prize Options/Names, P.O. Box 4710, Blair, NE 68009.

For a list of prizewinners (available after July 31, 1994) send a separate, stamped self-addressed envelope to: Million Dollar Sweepstakes Winners, P.O. Box 4728, Blair NE 68009.

The Extra Bonus Prize will be awarded in a random drawing to be conducted no later than 5/30/94 from among all entries received. To qualify, entries must be received by 3/31/94 and comply with published directions. No purchase necessary. For complete rules, send a self-addressed, stamped envelope (WA residents need not affix return postage) to: Extra Bonus Prize Rules, P.O. Box 4600, Blair, NE 68009.

SW9-92

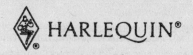
HARLEQUIN®

THE TAGGARTS OF TEXAS!

Harlequin's Ruth Jean Dale brings you
THE TAGGARTS OF TEXAS!

Those Taggart men—strong, sexy and hard to resist...

You've met Jesse James Taggart in FIREWORKS!
Harlequin Romance #3205 (July 1992)

Now meet Trey Smith—he's THE RED-BLOODED YANKEE!
Harlequin Temptation #413 (October 1992)

Then there's Daniel Boone Taggart in SHOWDOWN!
Harlequin Romance #3242 (January 1993)

And finally the Taggarts who started it all—in LEGEND!
Harlequin Historical #168 (April 1993)

Read all the Taggart romances!
Meet all the Taggart men!

Available wherever Harlequin books are sold.

WELCOME TO

The quintessential small town, where everyone
knows everybody else!

Finally, books that capture the pleasure
of tuning in to your favorite TV show!

Join your friends at Tyler in the eighth book, BACHELOR'S PUZZLE by Ginger
Chambers, available in October.

*What do Tyler's librarian and a cosmopolitan architect have in common? What
does the coroner's office have to reveal?*

GREAT READING...GREAT SAVINGS...
AND A FABULOUS FREE GIFT!

Each book set in Tyler is a self-contained love story; together, the twelve novels
stitch the fabric of the community. You can't miss the Tyler books on the shelves
because the covers honor the old American tradition of quilting; each cover
depicts a patch of the large Tyler quilt!

And you can receive a FABULOUS GIFT, ABSOLUTELY FREE, by collecting
proofs-of-purchase found in each Tyler book, *and* use our Tyler coupons to save
on your next TYLER book purchase.

If you missed *Whirlwind* (March), *Bright Hopes* (April), *Wisconsin Wedding* (May), *Monkey
Wrench* (June), *Blazing Star* (July), *Sunshine* (August) or *Arrowpoint* (September) and would
like to order them, send your name, address, zip or postal code, along with a check or money
order for $3.99 (please do not send cash), plus 75¢ postage and handling ($1.00 in Canada)
for each book ordered, payable to Harlequin Reader Service, to:

In the U.S.	In Canada
3010 Walden Avenue	P.O. Box 609
P.O. Box 1325	Fort Erie, Ontario
Buffalo, NY 14269-1325	L2A 5X3

Please specify book title(s) with your order.
Canadian residents add applicable federal and provincial taxes.   TYLER-8

HARLEQUIN®

Temptation®

the Fortune Boys

A funny, sexy miniseries from bestselling
author Elise Title!

**LOSING THEIR HEARTS MEANT
LOSING THEIR FORTUNES...**
If any of the four Fortune brothers were unfortunate
enough to wed, they'd be permanently divorced from
the Fortune millions—thanks to their father's last will
and testament.

**BUT CUPID HAD OTHER PLANS FOR
DENVER'S MOST ELIGIBLE BACHELORS!**
Meet Adam in #412 **ADAM & EVE** (Sept. 1992)
Meet Peter in #416 **FOR THE LOVE OF PETE**
   (Oct. 1992)
Meet Truman in #420 **TRUE LOVE** (Nov. 1992)
Meet Taylor in #424 **TAYLOR MADE** (Dec. 1992)

**WATCH THESE FOUR MEN TRY TO WIN AT
LOVE AND NOT FORFEIT $$$**